That's your lot.

That's your lot.

Limmy

HarperCollins*Publishers*

HarperCollins*Publishers*
1 London Bridge Street
London SE1 9GF

www.harpercollins.co.uk

First published by HarperCollins*Publishers* 2017

1 3 5 7 9 10 8 6 4 2

© Brian Limond 2017

A catalogue record of this book is
available from the British Library

ISBN 978-0-00-817260-2

Printed and bound in Great Britain by
Clays Ltd, St Ives plc

MIX
Paper from
responsible sources
FSC
www.fsc.org
FSC C007454

Contents

Pavement

George had a baby. A wee baby boy, called Sam. And he wanted to make his son proud. Proud of his old dad. You couldn't really make a baby feel proud of you, but George was thinking more about the future.

He wanted Sam to look back, when he was older, and think, 'I'm so proud of my dad. He was there for me and cared about me. That man there is my dad.'

George was out one day with Sam, pushing him in his pram, and he was thinking about all that. All that stuff about making his son proud. He was looking at his son's face looking back at him in the pram. Sam would look at George, then the sky and the people walking past. George wondered if Sam would ever remember all this, how much George was there for him.

Probably not. And that was a shame.

'Watch yourself, pal!' said somebody.

George stopped, and he saw a few workies looking at him. George had been walking on the pavement, and just a few feet in front of him was a new bit of pavement. The workies had been laying some fresh concrete, and it was still wet. The workie wanted to stop George before he went over it and left a mark.

'Thanks,' said George.

George had seen what happens when somebody went over wet concrete. You see it all around if you look for it. Walk around and you'll see bits of pavement with footsteps in them, or wheels from prams, or bikes, or some other mark made by people who didn't look where they were going.

Sometimes it was deliberate, though. Sometimes people wrote their name in it. George remembered that somebody had written their nickname outside the chippy where he grew up. It had been there for as long as he could remember. It was probably still there, and probably always would be. How was that for something to tell the grandweans?

Oh, and that got George thinking.

George watched the workies finish their work. He pretended to talk to Sam, as an excuse for hanging about. Eventually, some of them left in their council workie van, and some of them headed into a cafe nearby for their lunch.

George walked over to the edge of the wet concrete, and crouched down, like he was going to fetch something from the wee bag at the bottom of the pram.

Then he reached over to the concrete and began to write 'Sam'.

As he made the letter 'S', he thought about Sam in the future, coming to this very spot, with George. George would tell him that he wrote it there. And Sam would know that his old dad was mad about him, even back then. He'd know that when he was a baby, his dad was there for him and thinking about him. He'd bring his mates and point to the writing and say, 'That there was my dad.'

Just as George was beginning the letter 'A', a workie came out the cafe and asked George just what the hell he thought he was doing.

George said he was doing nothing. It was no use lying, though. He'd been caught red handed.

'I asked you what the fuck you think you're doing, mate,' said the workie.

George tried to turn the tables by making a big deal about the workie's swearing. He stood up and said, 'Here, don't you fucking swear in front of my wean. What's your name, you're getting reported.'

'Fuck yer wean,' said the workie, then he pointed at the writing. 'I'm gonnae have to lay that again.'

3

George couldn't believe his ears. He charged over to the workie, right over the concrete, and started shouting. 'What did you say? Fuck my wean, aye? Fuck my fucking ...'

The workie chinned him.

George punched him back, and the two of them fell onto the wet concrete.

The workie was much bigger, and held George's face down, then he shouted for his workie mates to phone the police.

The police eventually came, and tried to take George away, but they couldn't. The workie had been holding George's face in the concrete until the police turned up. Now the wet concrete was dry and rock solid, and the left side of George's face was stuck.

The police tried to talk to George, to calm him down, to tell him that they'd get him out, but he booted them away. He was fucking livid about how he was being treated as a criminal.

The police told him to go and fuck himself then, and they left him there. Then they took Sam back to his mum.

The next day, Sam and his mum came to visit George, to give him something to eat and drink, but mostly to tell him that he was a dummy. George didn't want Sam seeing him like that, and he didn't want to be told that he was a dummy, so he told her to fuck off.

So she did.

She came back a few days later. Then a few weeks later. Then she never came back at all.

George watched the years go by from down there on the pavement, as people offered him the leftovers from their kebabs or a drink from their half-finished bottles of beer. Somebody would sometimes put their jacket over him to keep him warm, but by the time he woke up the next morning, it had been stolen.

About ten years later, George saw Sam go by with his schoolmates.

One of his mates pointed at George and said, 'That's your dad!', and Sam laughed.

Sam didn't know it really actually was his dad, and neither did his mate. His mate just said it in the way that a person might point at a tramp and say, 'Oh look, there's your dad.'

Taxi Patter

Vinnie was down in London for a few days. Down from Glasgow. It was lovely weather down in London. It always was. He'd been down before, and even when the weather wasn't that nice, like if it was cloudy or pissing down, it was always better than whatever it was up the road.

Today, though, it was lovely, and all the Londoners were dressed for the occasion, with their T-shirts and shorts and bare legs.

When Vinnie got in a taxi, it was one of the first things the taxi driver mentioned.

'Lovely weather, isn't it?' said the driver.

'Aye,' said Vinnie. 'It's roasting.'

The driver smiled at Vinnie in the mirror. 'You from Scotland, yeah?'

'Aye, just down for the day.'

'Down for a spot of sightseeing?' asked the driver.

'Aye,' said Vinnie.

But that wasn't the truth. He didn't want to talk about it, because he knew he'd come across as stupid. He wasn't down for a spot of sightseeing, he was actually down for a concert. But he'd made an arse of it.

He was supposed to be seeing Art Garfunkel.

There was only one UK date on his world tour, and that was London, tonight. Or so Vinnie had thought. But it turned out it was last night.

Vinnie had found out when he got off the train. The second he got off, he saw an Art Garfunkel poster in the station, advertising the tour. He walked over to it, because he'd never seen the poster before, and because Art Garfunkel was the reason he was down. He saw that the London date was on Thursday, not Friday. And next to it were all these other dates.

He didn't know there were other UK dates. He'd only ever known about a tour from the Art Garfunkel forum. Somebody on the forum mentioned that the only UK date was in London.

But, looking back, they maybe just asked if Art's only UK date was London. They were maybe just asking, rather than saying that it was.

Or it could be that the person just said that they themselves were going to see the concert in London.

So Vinnie had gone ahead and searched for 'Art Garfunkel' and 'London', and up came the London date. Just London. And Vinnie took that as confirmation that Art was only going to be in London. So he booked it. Then he came all the way down from Glasgow to London, got off the train, and saw the poster with the dates.

And there on the poster was a date for Glasgow.

It had already passed, it was last Wednesday. Vinnie could have made it. He dearly would have loved to have made it. But now he wasn't going to see him in either Glasgow or London, and he felt so fucking stupid.

He loved Art Garfunkel.

Really, what a talented singer and songwriter.

Vinnie wasn't sure if it was Art who wrote all the songs in Simon & Garfunkel, but he must have. He was the main singer. Plus the fact that he left the band to go solo and then went on to write 'Bright Eyes', whereas Simon, the short one, disappeared without a trace. That tells you everything you need to know about Art.

Vinnie couldn't wait to see him live. But that just wouldn't be happening, not tonight anyway.

It didn't piss him off, though. He was used to it. He was used to things like this happening. But he couldn't laugh it off either. And he didn't want to go into it all with the driver.

9

So when the driver asked him if he was down for some sightseeing, he just said 'Aye'.

The driver nodded and started driving, looking out the window to the side. He wasn't looking at other cars, though. He was looking at the people on the pavement. And he'd turn his head all the way around to look at some of them.

'And what a day for it,' said the driver, looking at the people going by. 'D'you know what I mean?'

'Aye,' said Vinnie.

He thought he knew what the driver meant, but then the driver gave him a look in the mirror that made Vinnie think that he didn't know.

Vinnie asked 'For sightseeing?'

'Yeah,' said the driver. 'If you know what I mean.'

Vinnie didn't know what he meant, and it must have shown, because the driver looked at him again and said, 'The women.'

Vinnie got it now.

'Oh, right, right, aye,' said Vinnie. 'The lassies. The women. Aye.'

What the driver meant was the women. What he meant was, because it was a nice day, because it was lovely and warm, women were wearing less clothes. Instead of getting all wrapped up in big coats and pairs of tights, they were stripping down to keep cool. They were out in their bare legs or wearing thin clothes that let you see their bodies.

Vinnie got it. He looked out the window at them, and after a while, he started getting hard.

He was going to cover it up. He reached over for his bag, which was lying next to him on the back seat. He was going to pick it up and cover his bulge. But then he realised that it didn't matter, when he thought about it.

He left his bag where it was. Because when he actually thought about it, it was all right, when he thought about what the driver said.

He'd said it was a good day for sightseeing, a good day to look at women. To look at them and get turned on by them.

He wanted Vinnie to know that he fancied women, and he wanted to know if Vinnie fancied women as well, and the driver would like it if Vinnie did. For some reason.

Vinnie didn't know why the driver wanted any of that, but it didn't matter. Vinnie was fine with it, because he fancied women as well.

'Look,' said Vinnie.

The driver looked out the window to the side, to see what lassie Vinnie was talking about.

'Who?' said the driver, looking at Vinnie in the mirror, then he looked out the side window again.

'No,' said Vinnie. 'Look here.'

The driver looked in the mirror, down to where Vinnie's hands were, and saw that Vinnie had a hard-on. It was bulging underneath his tracksuit bottoms.

Vinnie saw the look on the driver's face, and it was like the driver didn't know what Vinnie was meaning. Vinnie thought that maybe the driver just thought his trackie bottoms were baggy and what he was looking at was just a big baggy bit raised in the air.

So Vinnie pulled the trackie leg tight to show the shape of his hard-on, so that the driver knew what it was and what Vinnie was talking about. But the driver still had that same look.

The driver even turned his head around to see it with his own eyes, in case he couldn't see it properly in the mirror, but he still had that same look. Vinnie smiled at him, but the driver looked away and didn't say anything.

What had happened?

Why did the driver act funny when Vinnie showed him his hard-on?

Was he gay?

Maybe that was it.

Maybe the driver was doing that thing that people do in taxis, the thing where the driver and the passenger say things that they're not really interested in, things like when you ask the driver what time he started and what time he finishes, or when the driver asks you if that's you on your way home now after a night out.

You know, taxi patter.

Vinnie had seen that being talked about on a stand-up comedy thing on the telly. Maybe the driver was just pretending to be into women, because that's just what you do. Vinnie sometimes pretended to be into football if the driver had football on the radio. He'd ask the driver who was playing and what the score was, even though he didn't care.

It's just taxi patter. It's just people pretending, but the driver got caught out. He fucked it up.

Vinnie sympathised, because he himself knew all about fucking things up. Just look at how he fucked up going to the concert, coming all the way down here when he could have went to the concert back in Glasgow.

He looked at the driver, and he could see that the guy look ashamed. He felt for him, so he decided to change the subject.

He leaned forward and put his hand on the driver's shoulder to let him know it was all right.

'Do you like Art Garfunkel?'

Grammar

Donnie started a new job, at an office. When he got there, he sent a group email to all the staff, introducing himself. It was a short and informal thing, nothing more than a few sentences. Most people replied saying hello back, putting in smileys or saying funny things in return. Some people didn't reply, but then they said hello in person later.

But this one person, called Toby, only replied to correct his grammar.

There was a bit in Donnie's email where he said 'should of' instead of 'should have'.

Toby had replied to it, copying everybody else in, to say: 'should *have*'.

Donnie thought of replying with something a bit cheeky, a bit funny, because he hoped that's how Toby meant it as well. He hoped Toby didn't mean it the way it came across, because the way it came across made Toby look a grumpy cunt that enjoyed embarrassing Donnie on his first day. And Donnie didn't want to work with somebody like that.

In the end, Donnie just replied with 'Oops. Thanks!'

He hoped for a jokey reply, something where Toby would say he was only joking, or maybe having a bad day. But he didn't get a reply.

Donnie wondered who Toby was, and he walked around the office until he heard somebody mentioning Toby's name. Donnie turned around and expected to see some kind of Oscar the Grouch, or some kind of anti-social Mr Bean. But Toby looked all right. He looked about 40, just an average sort of guy in a suit. He didn't look grumpy either. He was chatting to another member of staff, smiling away. And that made Donnie feel a bit better somehow.

A few days later, Donnie had to send another email around, this time something to do with work rather than introducing himself. This email wasn't for everybody in the office, but it was for a good number of them, and one of the people in the list was Toby.

Everybody replied normally, saying things like 'Good idea' or 'I think we should discuss this further.' But Toby replied again, simply to criticise Donnie's grasp of the English language.

Donnie had accidentally typed 'there' instead of 'their'.

The full sentence was 'We could cut the cost of printing their brochures if we print it at the same time as we print there pamphlets.'

And it was an accident.

Donnie knew the difference between 'there' and 'their', it was just a slip-up. He got the first 'their' right, so it was obviously just a slip-up, just a normal mistake that anybody could make. But there was Toby on it again, making Donnie look incompetent for the second time in his first week on the job.

Donnie just replied with 'Thank you, wordsmith.'

By replying with that, he wanted to gently suggest that Toby was being a smart arse, without it looking too sarcastic. It was Donnie's first week, after all. He didn't want to go in hard with the cheek when he'd barely got his feet under the table. But he also didn't want to be picked on. He wanted his reply to be just enough to put Toby off criticising him in the future, knowing that Donnie would fire back.

But as it turned out, Donnie wasn't being picked on. As time went on, Donnie discovered that Toby did it with everybody, all the time. But nobody else seemed to mind. They would either reply to the corrections with 'Thanks, Toby' or say nothing at all.

Nobody even seemed to bitch about him, not in front of Donnie anyway. If anything, they would defend

Toby, even if they were the victim of Toby's cuntish-ness. Like when Toby corrected Alice.

Alice had sent an email where she said the word 'colour's' instead of 'colours'. She was talking about the colours in the colour printer that they had up the back of the office, because it wasn't working properly. She'd said 'And there's something wrong with the colour's on all of the printouts.'

Toby had replied with 'The plural of colour is colours.'

Donnie asked Alice how she felt about that. It was verging on nasty, as far as Donnie was concerned. It was one thing to correct somebody's grammar, but another to type a reply like that.

Alice said that it was okay, because Toby corrects people's mistakes all the time. But Donnie said that there was a difference with this particular reply. It implied that Alice didn't just make a typo due to typing fast or autocorrect or losing concentration; it implied that she didn't know how to make a word plural, like she would make the mistake again because she just didn't know to do it, like she was in nursery school.

That's the impression that Donnie got, and he wanted Alice to be upset about it. But she wasn't. She just shrugged it off and said it was okay, and that it was a silly mistake anyway.

Donnie said that somebody should say something, but Alice said that it really was okay and that Toby was a nice guy. Just leave it.

Donnie tried to leave it, but when you're seeing somebody correcting everybody's grammar on a daily basis, you just want to say something. You just want to tell the guy to give it a rest with the corrections. What does it matter?

It's not as if the mistakes are being printed on the pamphlets and sent out, resulting in embarrassment for the company. It's not as if Toby was some kind of copy-editor or sub-editor, where it was his job to correct everybody's spelling and grammar before it went to print. He worked in accounts. His job was to do with numbers, not words. Just stick to your fucking job, mate.

Donnie tried to leave him alone, he tried to forget about him. He tried to ignore his ways.

He managed it for almost a month. He told himself that he wouldn't react or bitch or try to get anybody else bitching. He'd just be like everybody else and take no notice. Almost a month he managed it.

But then it all came out at the office party. They'd all booked a big table at a restaurant, and they all got drunk.

Donnie wasn't sitting near Toby, but he'd look over to Toby now and then, and try to listen in to his conversations. There was nothing interesting to listen to, but then Donnie heard something that he had to jump on.

He heard Toby say 'It depends who you send it to.'

It was a mistake!

'Wait!' shouted Donnie, pointing at Toby.

Toby didn't hear, but Alice did, and she stopped talking to see what Donnie was doing. It didn't look good to her.

'Toby!' shouted Donnie again, and Toby looked around to see Donnie smiling and pointing. When Donnie saw that he had Toby's attention, he asked him, 'What did you just say there?'

'What did I say when?' asked Toby, looking at everybody else.

To Donnie, Toby seemed sober, while he himself felt drunk. He knew he probably wouldn't fare well against somebody so alert, but this might be his only shot. It was too good an opportunity to miss. Even with the rest of the staff looking at him with their straight faces, looking concerned, he knew that they'd appreciate somebody just telling it like it is.

'What did you say when?' asked Donnie, grinning. 'What did you say when? I'll tell you what did you say when. You said, and I quote, "It depends who you send it to."'

Toby gave a confused smile, and searched the faces of everybody around to see if they were equally as confused. 'What on earth are you talking about?'

'Well,' said Donnie, raising his eyebrows. 'I'll tell you what on earth I am talking about. You said "It depends who you send it to." But should it not be something like "Depends to whom you send it"?'

Donnie was half out his seat, and somebody put their hand on his shoulder to gently put him back down. Some people were asking him to just leave it.

Toby wasn't smiling anymore. Donnie reckoned he looked caught out, that's what he reckoned. He looked caught the fuck out.

'I understand what you're saying,' said Toby. 'And you're right. But ...'

'Ahhhh!' laughed Donnie, pointing at Toby, looking at Alice, looking at everybody around, at his audience. 'I'm right. And therefore you are wrong! Ahhhh! Not so perfect after all, is he? Not so fucking perfect after all.'

Somebody said 'Don't, Donnie. Don't.'

But there was no way he was letting this one get away. And he knew that he spoke for everybody. For whatever reason, nobody wanted to say a thing, they were too polite. But Donnie knew it was doing their heads in, bottling it all up. Well, this was it. This was it.

'Seriously, Toby,' said Donnie. 'Seriously, mate. What's it all about?'

'What's what all about?' asked Toby. He looked at Donnie and the others. He tried to smile the confused smile from before, but it was without the same confidence. It was forced, and Donnie could see right through it. He had Toby on the ropes.

'The grammar thing. The spelling and the grammar thing, the fucking emails. Ever since day one. Ever since day fucking ...'

'Just leave it,' said Alice. 'Please.'

'No chance,' said Donnie.

'Look,' said Toby. 'I just think it's important that certain rules are followed, certain consistencies are kept so that ...'

'Depends who you send it to,' said Donnie, repeating Toby's mistake. 'Depends who you send it to. I don't think that's in the rule book. Let me just check ...' Donnie licked his thumb and leafed through an imaginary rule book and said 'Nope'.

'Sure,' said Toby. 'Sure. I take the point. But language evolves and ...'

'Oh!' shouted Donnie, his eyes lighting up. 'Oh! Did you hear that, everybody? Language evolves.'

'B-b-but,' stuttered Toby.

'B-b-but?' said Donnie, taking the utter piss. Alice stood up and walked away.

'But,' said Toby. 'Certain rules should be obeyed, or at least ...'

'But not by you, eh, Toby? By us, but not by you.'

'By all of us,' said Toby. 'S–s–so there's some consist-ency, so there's, there's, there's …'

'Why?' said Donnie, banging his hand on the table.

'Because,' said Toby, looking flustered as fuck. 'Because without, without knowing what, what, what …'

'Why?' said Donnie again, giving the table another bang. He looked at the people around him. They were neither joining in nor trying to stop him. They were looking down at their drinks in silence.

Toby stuttered on. 'Because … because … b–b–because …'

'Why?' asked Donnie, his eyes wide. 'Whyyyyyy?'

Toby stood up sharply, bumping the table with his legs and spilling the drinks around him. Then he shouted at the top of his voice.

'Because it's all I've got!'

The pub, which was previously loud with chatter, fell silent.

Donnie looked at the rest of the staff to see if this was some kind of act. He'd never seen somebody shout like that before, he thought people only snapped like that in soap operas or on a stage. Not in real life.

Donnie looked at them all, waiting for them to laugh. But none of them looked up from their drinks.

Toby spoke again, but this time, with the pub being silent, he only needed to whisper to be heard by everybody in there.

'It's all I've got.'

Toby picked up his coat from the back of his seat and left.

What Donnie didn't know, but what he found out later, was that Toby's wife and kids had died in an accident.

Stookie

Gerry had broken his arm. He fell in his back garden and landed in a bad way on the steps. He didn't think he'd broken anything, his arm felt intact. But the pain just wouldn't go away, even after a week. So he went to the hospital, where he found out that he'd broken the thing. It was a surprise. He didn't think he'd done that much damage, he expected there to be much more pain from a broken arm. But no, he'd broken it, and he'd need to wear a plaster cast.

A plaster cast.

Or a stookie, as they used to call it when he was wee.

He never had a stookie himself when he was wee, but every now and then, somebody would come into school with one on, usually on the arm. It was usually boys that got it, he couldn't remember any lassies wearing one, it was always the boys. That was maybe something to do with all the climbing about that boys did, all the climbing up drainpipes and trees, which lassies never seemed to do. He did sometimes see lassies wearing a kind of stookie, though. The soft ones that went around the neck. The cream-coloured ones made of foam. It made them look so stupid.

The nurse began putting on Gerry's stookie. It was a new experience for him, even just to watch. He didn't know how it was done. He had a memory of being in school and asking somebody how the stookie was put on, but he'd forgotten. He watched the nurse wrap the dry bandages around his arm. Then, when that was done, she began wrapping a wet bandage around. Wet with plaster.

He thought back to the lassies in school that used to wear the soft stookies around the neck, and wondered why they were always soft and never hard like a normal stookie. He wondered if a normal one would have made them look any less stupid.

God, he was such a cheeky cunt in school.

He couldn't remember the names or faces of the lassies he slagged off for wearing the neck thing, but he remembered doing it. He remembered how it made them look like dogs, when dogs have to wear that thing that stops them licking their stitches when they've had an operation. He used to love laughing at the lassies that had to wear one, and he loved the way they couldn't turn their neck for a quick comeback. It was funny saying something cheeky to them, then watching them have to turn their body all the way around to look at you because they couldn't turn their neck.

Guys didn't really get that type of slagging by having a stookie, though.

They were never laughed at, because having a stookie was almost something to be proud of. It was like a war wound. It meant you'd been up to stuff, something dangerous, and people would ask you what happened and how sore it was. Anybody that had their arm in a stookie would get all this respect, and people would cover the stookie in menshies.

There's another word he hadn't heard for years. Menshies. Mentions. People would write stuff on the stookie.

They'd write things like their name, or 'Get well soon', or write something funny. The rule was that you shouldn't write anything dodgy, even for a laugh, because then the person with the stookie would get into the trouble. The teacher would just end up asking who wrote the thing on the stookie, and the person who wrote it would be grassed up.

The nurse finished putting on the stookie, and told Gerry that he'd have to wait a short while in the hospital while the plaster dried.

As he waited, he thought about if he'd get his son to draw some menshies on it when he got home. Alex wasn't able to write yet, but he could draw some squiggles, or maybe get out his paints and paint some flowers. That would be nice. There was the potential for some embarrassment, going around with a stookie covered in daisies, but it would be a nice embarrassment.

Gerry remembered a boy from school.

There was one boy in school who came in with a stookie on. But he didn't get any respect. Nothing like it.

People wrote stuff on his stookie, but it was nothing nice. It was nothing but fucking horrible stuff, and he had to just take it. They'd hold his arm and then write all this horrible stuff on it. Nobody had any fear of being grassed on, because the boy knew what would happen if he grassed.

The nurse came and tapped on the stookie with her finger. She told Gerry that the plaster seemed to be dry enough now for him to leave, so he was free to go. He left the hospital and headed for the bus stop.

As he waited for the bus, he felt his arm begin to itch. He looked at his stookie, and thought back to that boy from his school.

He could barely remember the boy's name. It was maybe William. William McDonald or William

Campbell, one of these Scottish surnames – he wasn't sure. But Gerry remembered what was on the stookie. He looked at his own stookie and he could remember what was on William's stookie like it was right there in front of him. He remembered that there were lots of things written on it, lots of drawings as well, but biggest of all was the word 'TRAMP'.

The bus came and Gerry got on. He realised as he tried to get the change out of his pocket that things were going to be a lot harder with the stookie on. It was his right arm that was in the stookie, leaving his left arm free, but his change was in his right trouser pocket. Getting the change out of his right pocket with his left hand felt like he was using his left hand to shake somebody's hand when they were using their right.

'Hurry up,' he heard somebody saying on the bus. Somebody up the back.

He looked towards the voice, but he couldn't tell who said it. The bus was busy, with most of the people looking at him and the rest looking elsewhere. Nobody looked guilty.

The bus driver, who hadn't yet moved the bus away from the bus stop, stepped on the pedal and moved the bus away sharply. Gerry stumbled, and banged the stookie against one of the metal bars. It went *clink*.

Somebody laughed.

He heard a woman somewhere say something about how Gerry was going to break his arm again, or break the other one. A couple of other people laughed at that and said something else.

By the time the bus was slowing down for the next stop, Gerry still hadn't managed to get his money out. He took a step towards the bus driver and said, 'Sorry, I'll just …' meaning to say, 'I'll just be a second,' but the driver interrupted him.

'Give me it when you get off,' said the driver, pointing his thumb to the back of the bus. 'You're blocking the aisle. Move.'

'Thanks,' said Gerry, and he walked down the aisle.

He looked for a seat, but there weren't any. There was a guy up the back sitting next to a spare seat, but he had his bag on it. Gerry was sure the guy had seen him but was pretending that he didn't.

The bus got moving again, and Gerry held onto one of the metal bars so he didn't fall over. He glanced at a few people, and saw that some were still looking at him, even from close up. He looked away, and down to his stookie.

He kept his eyes there, on the stookie.

As he looked at it, he thought back to the stookie on William, and what was written. He remembered. He couldn't remember every word, but he could remember their shape, like he was looking at it on his stookie with half-closed eyes. He remembered how the word 'TRAMP' was written. They were in capitals, but the line on the letter p dropped down like a small p. It had looked too much like the letter D, so he drew the line down further to make it more like a p.

He remembered that it was him that wrote 'TRAMP'.

He wrote about half of the other stuff as well. He forgot that. He couldn't remember if he started it, but he wrote at least half of the stuff on that stookie, or told people what to write or what to draw.

He remembered that he drew a picture of William with flies around his head, like Pig Pen from Charlie Brown. He could see it on his own stookie, down near the fingers, down at the bottom right of the word 'TRAMP', near the line that came down.

Gerry looked away.

He looked up from his stookie and saw that he was being watched by a boy on one of the seats. He was maybe about six or seven, a couple of years older than Alex. Gerry looked down so that he wasn't staring back. He saw that one of the boy's socks was white, but the other was light grey.

A thought came to him. He never found out how William broke his arm.

Gerry looked at the boy's face again, and saw that the boy was now looking at the stookie. Gerry turned the stookie away quickly so that the boy couldn't see what was written there, before coming to his senses and remembering that there was nothing there.

The stookie began to make his arm itch again. His skin felt hot and sweaty.

He thought about getting home, and letting Alex draw some menshies on his arm. The idea didn't appeal to him as much as it did back at the hospital, but it was maybe because of being on the bus and how much his arm itched.

He looped his left arm around the bar that he'd been holding onto, his good arm, and poked the fingers under the stookie to give it a scratch, where it was itching. But he couldn't quite reach it.

And oh, it itched like fuck.

Keys

Gary had made a stupid mistake.

Him and Linda had a back garden, and at the back of the garden was their garden fence. It was a high wooden fence with a padlock on it, and behind the fence was a lane, where the bins were kept. The key for the padlock was on a keyring that also held a key for the back door of their house.

Gary had taken a bin bag out to the bins. He'd unlocked the padlock and left the key in the lock while he put the bag in the bin. But while he was there, he saw the bin for bottles and glass, and remembered that they had some bottles in the house that he'd like to bin as well.

He walked back through the gate, into his garden, and he was about to lock the padlock. But he decided not to. He didn't really have to. It was only a ten-second walk from the gate to the house. Did he really need to lock the padlock just for that? Maybe he would have if it wasn't for the padlock being rusty, which made it a pain in the arse to get the key in and out of. It could sometimes take almost a minute to lock and unlock it, and he couldn't be bothered with that.

So instead, he left the key in the padlock. He was sure it was safe. It wasn't as if somebody was going to rush up and grab the keys from the padlock during the ten seconds or so that he was away. But he had a look down the lane, just in case anybody was about to walk by. When he saw that nobody was there, he walked back to his house to get the bottles. If anybody managed to jump out from a hiding place and grab the keys from that rusty padlock in under ten seconds, well, they'd earned them.

He walked through the back door and into his kitchen where the bottles were. There were over a dozen of them, so he opened the cupboard under the kitchen sink, with the intention of getting one of the reusable bags to carry the bottles out to the bin.

But then his dad phoned, wanting some computer advice.

He wanted to know how to move a video off his phone and onto his computer, because his phone was running out of space. So Gary talked him through it.

KEYS

By the time he came off the phone, Gary had forgotten about the bottles, and he'd forgotten about the keys that he'd left in the padlock. He closed the door of the cupboard under the kitchen sink, without remembering why it was open in the first place.

The next day, Linda asked him to take the bottles out to the bin at the back, and that's when he remembered that he didn't get round to doing it the day before. He felt daft for forgetting to take out the bottles, but then the daft feeling was replaced with dread, when he remembered that he'd left the keys out there overnight.

He was about to tell Linda what had happened, but he hadn't yet checked to see if the keys were still there. There was no point in owning up to making such a stupid mistake if nothing bad had come from it. They had a spare key for the back door, so maybe it wasn't all bad. But it was. She'd know that somebody out there had the other key. Even if they didn't, even if the keys were still there, she'd know he left the back door unlocked overnight.

He'd check first. There was no point in sticking himself in it when he didn't need to.

He picked up the bottles in the house and put them in a bag, then carried them out to the gate. He could see that the gate was open, and he looked behind to see if Linda saw it as well. There would be questions if she saw that. But she wasn't looking.

From a distance, it looked like the keys were no longer in the padlock. That was a sight that he did not want to see, so he looked away until he got closer, hoping that when he got to the padlock, he'd see that the keys were there.

But the keys were gone.

He felt his heart begin to thump.

He was about to search the ground to see if the keys had dropped down, maybe with the wind blowing the padlock during the night, but first he had another look towards the house to see if Linda was looking. And thank fuck she wasn't.

He put down the bag of bottles and looked around in the pebbles that made up the path to the gate. While he was pushing the pebbles around, he was pushing the thought out of his head that somebody had stolen the keys. Somebody had stolen the keys from the padlock, which included the key to the back door. The back door to their fucking house.

He pushed the pebbles around some more, then looked in the same place over and over. He stood up and looked at the padlock. It was a pointless thing to do, and he knew it.

He took in a deep breath. He could feel his pulse in his temples.

This was bad. Seriously bad.

He remembered that he was supposed to be putting

bottles in the bin, and he was certain that if Linda didn't hear the sound of bottles crashing on top of bottles, she'd be wondering why. So he picked up the bag and emptied out the bottles. Then he had another look for the keys.

He looked at the grass in the lane, to see if the keys were there. He knew that he himself didn't drop them there, he definitely left the keys in the padlock, but maybe the person who took them from the padlock then dropped them in the lane accidentally. It was possible.

He got down on all fours, then looked at the lane from down low, hoping to see the shiny keys sticking up from the grass. But he couldn't see them.

He was going to have to tell Linda. He was actually going to have to tell her.

His throat tightened and his heart beat faster. He had to tell Linda that somebody had the key to their back door.

But he didn't want to. He really didn't want to.

It wouldn't just be a case of getting the lock in the door changed, because it wasn't as simple as that. The back door wasn't a normal door like that. They had fancy patio doors that they'd spent a fortune on, and the lock was part of the door. You couldn't just unscrew the lock and then put in a new one. If you replaced the lock then you'd probably have to replace the door as well, and that would cost a fortune. And he just did not want to tell Linda that. So he kept his mouth shut. He knew he was putting the security of their home at risk, but it was a risk worth taking for now, until he worked out what to do.

For now, he would just keep a lookout.

He spent the next few days looking out the window of the room that faced the back garden. The toilet window also faced the back garden, and after every visit to the toilet, he'd look out it, towards the gate and the lane behind.

One day he forgot to lock the toilet door. It was shut, but he had forgotten to lock it. After he washed and dried his hands, he had a look out the window. To do so was always an effort, because the window was high, and in order to look out it he had to step into the bath, and go on his tiptoes.

Linda walked in and saw him peering through the window, and asked him what he was doing.

He nearly fell in the bath. He said he wasn't doing anything, just looking out the window. He couldn't think of what else to say.

She looked through the window, and asked him if he was looking at their neighbour, Teresa.

He told her that Teresa wasn't there, but when he looked out, there she was, lying in her garden, reading a magazine.

When he pictured how it looked through Linda's eyes, it looked bad. He looked like an old-school pervert.

Linda walked away, and Gary was about to call her back to say that it wasn't what she thought. But he knew that if she asked what it was he was looking at, he'd probably have to tell her that he left the keys in the padlock and now they were gone. Maybe he would have owned up if she kept at it, but because she walked away, he just left it.

A week passed, with no break-ins. It surprised Gary, especially considering that they'd left the house unoccupied for a few hours here and there at various times of the day.

There was even a time when they went through to Linda's mum and dad's for the night, and they'd made it quite obvious that they weren't home. Gary tried hard to not make it so obvious, by leaving all the lights on and turning on the radio. Linda asked him why he was doing that, considering he didn't usually. He told her that there was no right or wrong time to start being conscious of burglars. But she said that she doubted that anybody would be able to break in, not with all the locks they had. There were locks on the windows, and there were the special locks on the front and back doors. Multipoint locks. Burglars couldn't kick their way past those.

'But somebody could pick them,' said Gary.

Gary wasn't sure if it was a clever move to continue with the talk of burglars, or a stupid one. It would be a stupid move if the burglars chose that night to break in, on the day that Gary coincidentally became conscious of burglars. She would have asked him if he was psychic, especially because he also seemed to predict that the burglars got into the house by apparently picking the lock. Then she'd maybe wonder if they had a key. Then she'd ask Gary where the keys were, and she'd see that one of them was missing. And she'd see the look on his face. And he'd have to tell her how long he'd known for. And she'd know he let her think that he was perving on Teresa, rather than just owning up to the truth.

'Och, forget it,' said Gary, switching off the lights. 'You're right.'

He switched off every light in the house. He didn't even close the curtains. He'd rather that the house looked unoccupied and ripe for the picking, than face the music. He'd rather jeopardise their telly, their computers and anything else worth stealing. He'd rather do that and take all the hassle that it would cause, all the phone calls and changing of passwords and proving who he was, than face the music. He could face it eventually, but he wanted some more time to try and work it all out and make things right.

They left the house, and Gary spent the night thinking about what they'd be returning to the next day.

But when they returned, everything was intact.

Gary looked around the house at all the things worth knocking. The telly, the computers, even the food in the fridge. Linda watched him as he looked at it all.

He saw her watching and said, 'Ah, good to be back. It's just good to be back.'

After that night, Gary told himself that if burglars were going to break in, if they truly had their eyes on the house, they would have broken in then. And because they didn't, then maybe there weren't any burglars. Maybe the keys weren't really in the hands of a thief, and they were lying out there in the pebbles after all.

He took a walk to the gate and had another look, making sure again that he wasn't spotted by Linda. He looked in the pebbles and the grass, and in the path behind the gate, but there was nothing. It was puzzling.

Perhaps somebody did snatch the keys, but the type of person that did such a thing would be out their face at the time, and they've since forgotten where the keys came from. Perhaps there was a thief somewhere out there, wondering whose keys were in his pocket.

Gary took off the padlock and threw it in the bin, and told himself to remember to buy a new one, so that Linda didn't ask questions. He also reminded himself to get a copy of the key to the back door, because if they lost the one they had left, Linda would ask what happened to the other one. And she'd see the look on his face. Then she'd find out about how he left the keys in the padlock, and that he left the house unoccupied with all the lights off and the curtains open, putting everything at risk.

Gary went to the shops and replaced the padlock. He got an extra key cut for the back door, and put them on a keyring that looked just the same as the old one. Linda didn't suspect a thing.

Everything was going to be all right. Linda had been a bit funny with him since the perving incident with Teresa, but with regards to the keys, everything was going to be all right.

Then, a few days later, while Gary was looking out the bedroom window upstairs, he saw a guy cycling about outside in the street. There was something about him that Gary didn't like the look of.

The guy wasn't wearing cycling clothes. He was wearing denims and a jacket, and he wasn't wearing a helmet. That would usually be unremarkable, because you don't have to have all the bright clothes and a helmet to ride a bike. But usually, the only people you saw without a helmet were younger guys on a BMX. But this guy was about 30 years old, and he was cycling on a mountain bike that looked dodgy. The bike looked featureless, it was completely black with no logo, like it had been spray-painted black. And why was that? Because it had probably been knocked, and probably by the guy himself.

The guy went up the street, past the house. But when he got a few doors up, he doubled back.

Gary stepped away from the window to look out the side of the curtain, so that he couldn't be seen. He saw the guy look at a few houses, which gave Gary some relief, because it didn't look like the guy had an interest in Gary's house in particular. But as the guy cycled past Gary's front gate, he turned his head quickly to look at the living-room window. And he kept looking at it, even as he passed the houses further down the street.

It was him.

He was the man with the keys.

Gary knew what was coming. It was at that point that Gary thought that he really should tell Linda. He should tell Linda the fucking truth. He should tell Linda that he was sorry, he was so fucking sorry, but he'd left the keys in the padlock around the back, and now there was a guy casing their house. They should go to the police. They were about to get everything stolen.

But it would cost a fortune to get that lock replaced.

And it wasn't just that either. It was the fact that he caused it. And then lied about it. Plus he'd left the house unoccupied, with the lights off and curtain open, knowing that they could have had their computers stolen. Plus there was the thing with Teresa. Him and Linda had been heading for the rocks ever since that happened, and he could have turned it around with a truthful explanation, but instead of that he just let it happen.

A couple of days passed, with no sight of the guy on the bike. But Gary knew the guy was out there, just biding his time. All it would take was one more night away from home.

'We're going through to my mum's and dad's tonight,' said Linda.

But he made every excuse to not go.

He told her he didn't feel well, his head was killing him. But she said he could just take a couple of pain-killers and lie in bed when he got there.

He told her that didn't like her dad, which was partly true. He told her that he didn't like the way her dad patted Gary's belly almost every time he went over, making a comment about Gary 'putting on the beef'. But Linda just told him to get over it, or say something back, or lose weight.

He told her that he didn't like her mum either.

Gary and Linda fell out, and she went through to her mum's and dad's by herself. He felt bad, but there was no alternative, none that he could think of.

He slept in the house that night with every light on. He balanced a brush against the patio door in the kitchen so that it would fall over and hit the tiles if the door was opened. He tested it and it made a clatter that he could hear from anywhere in the house.

The night passed with no break-in, and Gary waited for Linda to come home the next day, but she texted him to say that she'd be staying for not one night but two.

Gary saw the guy on the bike again while she was away, this time cycling down the path behind the house. Gary could only see the top of the guy's head, but he saw the head slow down near his gate, before speeding up and cycling off.

He felt like phoning the police, but he didn't. It was just too late now.

He could have just phoned them or gone over to the station and asked them to keep things confidential. It might have been enough for the police to get a description of the guy. They might have known who Gary was talking about and paid the guy a visit, which would have scared the guy off. He'd maybe get the keys back.

But he didn't do any of that. He just wanted it all to go away.

When Linda returned, she said she was going to sleep on the couch, in the living room. She reckoned that was her and him finished.

He could've just told her then. He could have told her that he left the keys in the padlock out in the gate, that he wasn't shagging Teresa next door or looking at her or whatever it was that Linda thought was going on. He could have said he was sorry for leaving the house unoccupied, and hope that she understood why he lied.

He may as well have just told her the truth, if she reckoned that was her and him finished. There was nothing to lose. But he didn't. He still had hope that it would work out somehow.

Then, one night, while he was lying awake upstairs in bed and she was sleeping downstairs in the living room, he heard the brush hit the tiles.

If there was a time to come clean, that was it.

Everything worth stealing was in the living room. The telly, the stereo, and probably the tablet. All the stuff worth knocking was in the living room, and the burglar probably knew that. They probably learned all about that in jail.

All he had to do was run downstairs and chase away the burglar.

But then Linda would ask questions, and she'd see the look on his face.

Trophies

Martin was a cobbler. But like most cobblers, he didn't just mend shoes. He cut keys. He did engravings. He engraved things like trophies and medals and name-plates for doors. People could either come in with the nameplates to be engraved, or they could pick one of the ones he had for sale on the shelves.

He also had trophies and medals for sale, which sat on the shelf above the nameplates and door knockers. It made the wall look like something you'd see in a football club, like a trophy cabinet. Martin used to make a joke about it with customers who were in to get their shoes fixed.

They'd point to their shoes and ask him, 'Are you able to fix this? Is that something you do?'

And he'd say, 'I do that. And you willnae find anybody better. Just look at my trophies!'

But he didn't bother making that joke anymore.

The door beeped, and in walked a customer. Martin gave him a quick look up and down. Right away, he didn't like the look of the guy. A possible thief, thought Martin. The guy looked shifty. It was the way he didn't walk up to the counter to be served, but instead chose to hover around the things nearest the door.

Martin would get cunts like him in now and then. It was a busy street outside. They'd come in and hover about. Martin would turn his back on them for a second, then he'd hear the door beep and the guy would be gone. They'd have grabbed something from the rails, something worthless, like a packet of heel protectors. Martin could sometimes tell what they'd grabbed because they'd have grabbed the item off the rail so quickly that it would cause the remaining packets on the rail to swing.

And that's what this guy was like. Hovering about. He didn't look like he was browsing. If a person was browsing, they'd usually browse around just one type of item. They'd maybe browse around the items for doors, like the door knockers and nameplates, or browse around the trophies and medals – but they'd never drift from the door items to the trophies, like this guy was doing. Nobody ever came into his shop for a nameplate and a trophy, it was either one or the other.

This guy was a thief. He was just waiting for Martin to turn his back, then he'd grab something shiny, and out the door he'd go. He'd be off with the heel protectors, thinking that they were made of solid gold, and he'd go around the pubs trying to sell them.

'Can I help you?' asked Martin.

That was the line that normally caused these cunts to leave. They'd say nothing in reply, like they hadn't heard you, then they'd leave a few seconds later when they realised there was no way you were taking your eyes off them.

The guy looked at Martin and said 'Yeah', in that posh way. He played with his fingers, like an awkward teenager. It could be that he wasn't a thief, but just shy, and he didn't know how to ask for what he wanted. You couldn't be sure, though, not yet.

The door beeped as another man entered the shop. He was wearing denims and a suit jacket, and was pulling a shoebox out of a large paper bag. Martin didn't like two people in the shop at the one time. The guy with the shoebox was less likely to be a thief than the first guy, but he couldn't ask the first guy to leave.

'We're shut,' said Martin.

'Shut?' asked the man, looking at the other guy. 'But …'

'I said we're shut.'

The man didn't like the attitude. 'Fuck off, then.'

'You fuck off.'

The man opened the door and left. The other guy decided to leave as well, slipping out before the door closed over.

Good. Fuck off. Pair of cunts.

You know, he used to joke about all the trophies on the wall being like a trophy cabinet, like he'd earned them. It was obviously a joke, but these cunts wouldn't even crack a smile. But see seriously? All joking aside? He fucking deserved a trophy, for the cunts he had to put up with in there.

New Life

Alan had gathered all his mates and a few family members at his flat. His girlfriend Lisa was there as well. It was a surprise. There was going to be an announcement, he said. Not even Lisa knew what it was about. It wasn't his birthday or anything.

They came into the flat, smiling and asking questions. They were to be there at 7 p.m. Some of them had asked what they were to wear, but Alan had told them that it didn't matter. Just wear what you want, it was nothing fancy, they weren't going out clubbing. It was just an announcement.

'What do you mean when you say you're going to make an announcement?' asked Lisa throughout the week.

'Just wait, you'll see,' said Alan.

Alan seemed more upbeat lately than he had been for quite some time. Whatever the announcement was, it was good to see him like that. Lisa wondered if it was a new job, but would he really get everybody around just to announce that?

Everybody arrived and chatted for a few minutes while Alan took their coats and got them drinks. Alan's best mate Steven said it was like one of those murder mystery weekends you hear about, but Alan said it was going be nothing like that, don't get your hopes up.

They were enjoying it, though. Steven said he liked it, whatever it was, and Alan said he did as well. It was exciting and he was glad he came up with the idea.

Alan walked into the middle of the living room where everybody was, and stood on the rug in front of the telly. He cleared his throat in the jokey way that a person does when they want to make a speech.

'Oh,' said Anne, another one of Alan's pals. 'Here it is.'

'The announcement,' said Lisa. 'At last.'

She really didn't know what this could be. It could only be a good thing. All of this was a good thing. Alan rarely came up with an idea by himself, but it wasn't his fault. He'd been struggling for a while, with everything.

'So,' said Alan. 'Here it is.'

He looked nervous. Lisa asked him if he wanted to sit down, but he said that he was fine. He was just trying to think of how to get this across, the thing he had to say.

'So,' he said again. 'As you know, I've had … no, in fact, first of all, thanks for coming, everybody, let me just say that first.'

'You're welcome, mate,' said Steven.

Alan nodded and got back into it.

'Right,' said Alan. 'So, as you know, I'm prone to getting a bit down.'

The happy atmosphere in the room subsided. The smiles were still there, but their eyes were no longer smiling. They began to realise that the thing that Alan had to say was a bit more serious than they first thought.

He turned the wrist of his right hand around to face everybody. There was a scar on it. 'And you all know about this.'

Lisa looked at everybody in the room, and saw that they were becoming uncomfortable. Chris, one of Alan's cousins, turned his head away to look at the wall to his side, even though there was nothing there of interest.

'Alan,' said Lisa. 'What is this?'

'It's fine,' he said. 'It's fine. It's all right, everybody.'

He smiled at everybody until he got a smile back. Then he continued to talk.

'You all know about it,' he said. 'I've spoken to you all. You know how hard I've tried, you know I've tried everything. Pills, counselling, everything. I've tried everything. And it worked, for a while. But there I was again. On Monday, I think.'

This was the first time that Lisa had heard anything about Monday. 'There you were again what?' she asked. 'What happened on Monday?'

Alan took a deep breath and just came out and said it. 'I was about to kill myself.'

'Jesus,' said Steven.

'For God's sake, Alan,' said Cheryl, sympathetically. She gave Lisa's back a rub.

Lisa put her face in her hands and was instantly in tears.

'I was up at the Erskine Bridge,' said Alan. 'I walked all the way up there. Took me over an hour. I walked all the way up there and I was going to throw myself off. And I knew that if I did, that was it.'

He looked at his wrist.

'No going back this time,' he said. 'You step off that bridge, it's over. No ambulance, no rushing to the hospital. You step off there, and it's over. Doesn't matter how much you change your mind on the way down, it's over.'

'Shut up,' said Lisa from behind her hands. 'Just shut up.'

'We better leave,' said Cheryl to everybody else, standing up. 'We should go. Come on.'

'No,' said Alan. He looked at everybody and smiled. 'Because this is what I want to say. I've got something to say. I swear this will be the last time that you'll hear me talk about this. Will you hear me out?'

Cheryl looked at him and everybody else. Lisa looked up from her hands and waited for Alan to speak. Cheryl sat down and started rubbing Lisa's back again.

Alan had been standing on the rug, but now he felt like sitting. He pulled over a small table that was behind him, then he sat down on it and began to speak more quietly. He realised that although he was feeling good, he was potentially causing pain to the others, so he didn't smile, even though he wanted to.

'I don't know why I want to die,' he said. 'I don't really know. But I know that I don't enjoy my life. I've gone too far into a life that I don't like, and I just want it all to end.'

He looked at Lisa.

'But as I was up there on the bridge, it dawned on me that I didn't want to end my life, not completely. I just wanted to end this one, if that makes sense. I think I could enjoy life, if I was somebody else.'

'Then be somebody else,' said Lisa. 'Do whatever you want. Leave if you want to. I'd rather you were somewhere else than here and wanting to jump off the fucking …'

She broke down again. Cheryl gave her back a rub and kissed her head.

'I thought about that,' he said. 'I thought about it on the bridge. I thought about just running away. Just getting some money and getting on a plane and going to Canada or somewhere and starting again. But that would cost a ton of money. It would cost a serious ton of money, and I'd have to find somewhere to live and get my head around it all and think about all the forms and, oh, I don't know. There's always something. There's always something.'

He rubbed his head.

'I want to stay here, but I just want everything to be different. I want to be home, but with different faces and places, doing different things with different … I really don't know. I know that it all sounds like it won't change a thing. It doesn't make a lot of sense to me now, but it made sense to me when I was up on the bridge, and I'm not going to go back up there to try and remember. I told myself I was going to do it and that's why I asked you here and I'm going to do it. I have to.'

'Do what?' asked Steven. He looked at Alan's hands to see if he was holding a razor, in case Alan's plan was to cut his wrist or his throat, right in front of them all. But there was no razor.

'Please don't feel bad,' said Alan. 'But I told myself that if I don't then I'd end up killing myself and I'd never see you again anyway. You'd lose me anyway.'

Anne didn't get it. She looked at Lisa and she could see that Lisa didn't get it either. Neither did Cheryl or anybody else. Anne looked to Alan and said, 'Alan, I don't think anybody knows what you mean.'

Alan took another deep breath and tried to remember how much sense it made on the bridge, then he said it.

'After you leave here tonight, you don't know me. After tonight, my name will be Craig.'

There was quiet in the room as they thought about what he could mean. Steven asked, 'What do you mean? You're changing your name?'

'No,' said Alan. 'Well, aye. But not just the name.' He took a breath and tried to keep it simple. 'After tonight, I'll be a guy called Craig.'

Before they left, Alan told them the best way to go about it all. The technicalities. The dos and don'ts. He'd thought it all out.

Lisa was heartbroken, and asked him if he was joking. She wanted him to tell her he was joking. She said it must be a joke and she wouldn't go through with it, but he explained again that it was either this or he was going up to that bridge. If they spoke to him again, he'd be found the following day, floating face down in the Clyde, and that was a promise.

They left, and for the following couple of weeks, they never saw him.

Then, they did.

They started to see him around. They'd get a glimpse of him, then he'd be gone for a month. He'd be passing by as a passenger on a bus, or he'd be seen coming out of a building or getting into a car. Lisa had never seen him herself and wanted every detail about who he was with and what he was doing.

Anne saw him in a park. He was with a group of people, studenty types. One of them had a guitar, and they had a tightrope tied between a couple of trees. They were people like that. They were the type of people that Alan used to laugh at, but Anne said he looked like he was having a good time.

Steven saw him in a club. Steven was with a lassie he'd just met, a lassie he'd got dancing with. She said she wanted to introduce him to her mates, and she led Steven towards a table. One of her mates was Craig. Steven and Craig had said 'Pleased to meet you' to each other, like it was the first time they'd met. Steven stood around for a minute, to pretend that everything was normal, then he told the lassie that he had to go to the toilet. He took a detour to the cloakroom, got his jacket and left. It was too much.

Lisa was worried that she'd never see Craig again after that, that he'd move away or be found face down in the Clyde like he promised.

But then she finally saw him, in Lidl.

There was something different about him. Nothing much, but something. His hair was a bit longer at the top than the last time she saw him. The denims he was wearing were a darker shade of blue than he usually wore, but that was nothing much. He was wearing a jumper, and that was something.

He walked past her, but she didn't look at him, not directly. She watched his reflection on the metal edge at the front of the shelf. He might have turned his head to look at her, but she couldn't be sure. Then he was gone.

She saw him in there again a week after that. And then a few days after that.

The last time she saw him, he walked around the aisles for ten minutes, but then only left with a couple of packets of crisps.

The next time they were in, she would smile at him.

Or she might just go ahead and talk to him. She thought it would be all right, because it wasn't like she'd be talking to Alan. She wouldn't be talking to him as Alan. She'd be talking to Craig. She liked the guy. And you read things about supermarkets, about how that's where some couples first meet.

Moustache

There was an explosion.

Frank had been walking to the job centre. To get there, Frank would usually leave his house and stay on that side of the street for ten minutes, walking past the tenements, past the community centre and the factory. Then there would be more tenements, and when he reached those, he'd cross over to the job centre.

It was when he reached the factory that the explosion happened.

When it happened, in that first instant, he didn't know that it was an explosion. He didn't know if it was something that had happened inside him, like a heart attack or a stroke, or something that had happened outside his body, out in the open. Whatever it was, the combination of the sound and the force made him fall on his side and bang his head on the ground.

His eyes were shut and his ears were ringing. He couldn't see or hear anything, but he could smell dust. It reminded him of whenever he walked past the flats over in Finnieston, the ones that were being demolished, and the dust that blew onto the street. The smell told him that the thing that had happened hadn't just happened to him, it was no heart attack. He knew that when he opened his eyes, he was going to see something.

He opened them slowly and narrowly, so that the dust he could smell wouldn't go in his eyes.

He looked in front of him. Through the dust he could see that it was like half the factory and the surrounding tenements were lying on the road. There were twisted sheets of corrugated iron, there was broken glass and broken window frames. Strewn across the road were building bricks from the factory, and large blocks of sandstone from the tenements. The scene looked like a sandcastle that had been kicked across a beach.

There had been an explosion at the factory.

Frank checked himself, his arms and legs, and saw they were intact. He looked towards the rubble in front of him, and waited for the dust to clear.

It was quiet. He thought he had been deafened, but he realised he wasn't when he heard the first scream. People had been shocked into silence. But after the first scream, others began to follow.

There was a rumble, then the sound of something crashing to the ground, either a building or part of one. People screamed and shouted again. A mix of women and men.

Frank looked at his arms and legs again and gave them a squeeze, to double check that they were fine. When he was sure that they were, he got to his feet, and began to walk diagonally across the road.

A few people ran past him, some heading the way he was heading, and some heading back the way he came. A guy in his forties, around the same age as Frank, emerged from the dust. He had blood on his head. He stopped to look Frank up and down, then he rubbed his eyes and carried on walking.

Frank walked forward towards the sounds of people shouting, people speaking, or the sound of anything moving, anything that sounded like it was being moved by somebody trying to free themselves from the disaster.

He heard the sound of a female voice, and he began jogging towards it. He found a woman lying underneath one of the sheets of corrugated iron. She was wearing a blue coat, that was either light blue or looked light blue because of the dust. The sheet she was under didn't look like it had either hurt her or pinned her down. She was crawling away from underneath it.

Then he heard a boy's voice, groaning.

Frank looked towards the direction of the voice, then looked at the woman. She looked like she'd able to sort herself out, but he'd come back after finding the boy.

He ran towards the boy's groaning until he found him. He was with another boy. Both of them looked around 12. They were on the ground at opposite ends from each other, like when two boys of that age share a bed but don't want to be face to face.

One was sitting up, and the other was leaning on an elbow, as both of them pushed away the broken wood that had landed on their legs.

Frank could see that they were both able to move their legs and feet. One was smiling. The other was in pain, but judging by his face, it looked like the pain was nothing much, on a par with grazing a knee or banging a shin.

He was about to head back to the woman when he heard panting.

It was the sound of a man in a lot of pain, breathing through his teeth, quickly. Then it stopped, then started again.

It came from the right, towards the factory. Looking in that direction, Frank could see a flashing yellow light, which he thought was the light from a fire engine or some other emergency service. But then he saw that the yellow light was coming from flames. Through the dust, he could see that the factory was on fire.

Frank walked in that direction slowly. There was more rubble. It became higher, and the dust cloud was thicker.

'Hello?' shouted Frank. But the man didn't shout back, he only panted and coughed.

Frank walked towards the sound, until he saw a hand sticking out from the rubble. Then he saw the guy's legs. They were trapped, but in a far worse way than the boys. The legs were underneath a short but heavy-looking beam of wood, and they looked broken. One of the legs was bent in the wrong direction at the knee.

He followed the legs with his eyes to try and find the guy's face. He heard the panting again. They were short breaths. The breaths of a man trapped under the weight of the rubble, making every breath an effort.

He leaned over and began to lift one of the rocks away from the rubble, but then stopped when he saw that the guy was one of those guys with the funny moustaches. The type of moustache that curled up at the side like Poirot or an old-fashioned boxer.

Frank liked people like that, usually, these cartoony types with their funny moustaches or big beards or bow ties, the ones that treated life like it was one big fancy-dress party.

But now wasn't the time. There had been an explosion, and people needed help.

He put the rock back down and ran back to the woman from before, to make sure she had got out from beneath the corrugated iron.

He found her as she was getting to her feet with the help of another man who was taking her arm. Frank took her other arm.

'Thanks,' she said. 'My God, what happened? What was it?'

'It was that factory,' said Frank, pointing towards the flames. 'There was a factory there.'

The other guy spoke to Frank. 'Is there anybody else?' he asked. 'Back there?'

'Aye,' said Frank. 'There were a couple of boys over this way.'

Frank and the other guy guided the woman to the pavement at the other side of the road, then they rushed back onto the road to help the boys.

One of the boys was already on his feet. His denims were ripped and Frank could see a graze on the legs through the hole, but he looked like he got away with it. He was very lucky, relatively speaking. The other boy looked like he was in more pain, holding his hip.

'How's your leg, son?' asked Frank. 'Is it your hip? Do you think you could get up?'

The boy got up quickly after Frank spoke to him, like he wasn't really in that much pain and all it took was a grown man to snap him out of his childishness.

The boy's pal helped him up, and Frank and the other guy stood by, ready to help if need be. But the boys were fine, and off they went, with the luckier one of the two helping the other one limp away.

The man asked Frank 'Anybody else?' as he looked around. 'Who else?'

Frank looked towards where the boys had headed.

'Boys!' shouted Frank, into the cloud of dust.

'What?' shouted one of them.

'Did you see anybody else?' asked Frank. 'Any of your wee pals missing?'

'No,' came the voice.

'All right,' shouted Frank.

The other man looked around, standing on the spot, swivelling to the left and right, to see or hear anything.

They heard a conversation from somewhere in the cloud of dust.

A lassie said, 'What are you looking for?'

A woman said, 'My phone.'

Frank ran off in that direction, to help this woman find her phone. She'd need it to let her family know she was all right. But he'd have to be fast. It wouldn't be long until the police came and cleared everybody away and taped the area off, and if she didn't find the phone before that happened, it would probably be lost for good. He'd help her find that and anything else that was missing, he'd see if anybody else was missing anything, then he'd come back to check on the guy with the funny moustache, if there was time.

Porridge

Jason sat at the kitchen table, eating his breakfast. It was the same breakfast he'd had every day for the past three months. It was a bowl of porridge, made by his wife Mary.

He didn't like it.

His favourite cereal was Frosties, but he wasn't allowed to have that anymore. He'd been stuffing his face too much recently, not just with Frosties but with everything, and Mary blamed it on what he was having for breakfast.

She told him that what was happening was that he was starting the day with a sugar rush. He was starting the day on a bad foot. Then he'd come crashing down an hour later, and crave more sugar. She said that was why he was snacking throughout the day, eating chocolate and crisps and whatever else he bought at the shops on his way to work. It was why he was fat and always tired.

So it would be porridge now. And he wasn't even allowed salt in it either, because salt was bad for you. It would be porridge oats and hot water, with a splash of milk on top, if he wanted.

Soy milk.

That was how he started every day. Every single day. He'd go to bed, knowing that the next day would start that way. And in the morning, he could barely bring himself to climb out of bed.

He couldn't take it.

He asked her if he could maybe have Frosties as a weekend breakfast treat, as a wee reward for managing to stay off it during the week.

But she said no and told him to stick with it, he'd thank her in the end.

He told her he understood that she was trying to do a good thing, but he asked her to consider if it was any kind of life to deprive yourself of the things you like, just for the sake of being a few pounds lighter or having a bit of extra get up and go.

But she told him he was fat and tired, how was that any kind of life?

He said all right, all right, he'd do it, and he asked her how long it would last. A couple of weeks? A month? Or was it when he got down to a certain weight? He could do it as long as he knew that there was light at the end of the tunnel.

She said that there was no reason for it to end. 'You'll get used to it,' she said. But he never did. And it was driving him out of his mind.

But then, one morning, something happened.

'Look at this,' he said, holding up a spoonful of porridge that he'd just lifted out from his bowl.

'What is it?' she asked.

'Come around here and look.'

'What is it?' she asked again. 'It isnae a fly or something is it? If it is, I don't want to see it.'

'No,' he said. 'Just come here and look. It's funny.'

'Funny?' she asked.

She wondered what could possibly be funny about porridge, so she stood up and walked around to his side of the table. She looked into the bowl of porridge, and then at the spoon. There was nothing funny there.

She asked: 'So what is it?'

Jason raised the spoon and turned it slightly. 'D'you not think that looks a bit like Charlie?'

She began walking away, without looking at the spoon. She couldn't be bothered with this.

'Look!' said Jason, smiling.

She stopped and turned. Curiosity got the better of her. She walked back to Jason's side, knowing that it was a waste of time. But she was curious.

She looked at the spoon, ready to say 'No' and walk away. But you know what?

'It does!' she said.

She leaned closer to it, and tilted her head from side to side to view it from different angles. She laughed. 'It actually does!'

She looked for her phone to take a picture, she was going to send it to Charlie's wife Deborah. But she couldn't find it.

Jason smiled at the porridge on the spoon, then pointed at one bit with his pinky. 'Do you see that bit there? That's his hair. Do you see it? How much does that look like Charlie's hair?'

'I know,' she said. 'It's the spitting image.'

And it was. It was the double. Charlie had thick, wiry fair hair that looked all wavy and bumpy like a cloud. Or like a lump of porridge.

Mary looked at it for a while longer, then she lost interest.

She walked back around to her side of the table and sat down. And it was back to business as usual, as quickly as that. George went back to eating his porridge. They finished their breakfast, left the house, got into their separate cars and went away to work.

A few days later, something else happened.

Mary read about it when she and Jason were having breakfast. Deborah had posted an update on Facebook.

'Oh my God,' said Mary, looking at her phone. 'Did you see the news? Are you friends with Deborah? On Facebook?'

'No,' said Jason, looking concerned. 'What news? About Deborah?'

He paused the telly and waited for her to speak, but she looked lost in thought, trying to get her head around something.

'Mary,' said Jason. 'What is it? What's wrong with Deborah?'

'It's not Deborah,' said Mary. 'It's Charlie.'

She looked at her phone again in disbelief, then looked at Jason with her mouth open. 'You remember we saw Charlie in the porridge?'

'Charlie in the what?' asked Jason. 'Oh that. That bit of porridge that looked like Charlie? What about it?'

'He crashed his motor.'

Jason's eyes widened. 'What? Is he all right? He's not fucking dead, is he?'

'He's fine,' she said, looking at her phone. 'But it could have been a lot worse. There was some kind of fault, but it happened just as he left the house.' She blew through her mouth. 'Imagine he was on the motorway.'

Mary looked up from her phone to Jason, but he was looking at his porridge.

She said: 'Did you hear me?'

'Aye,' he said, still looking at the porridge. And then: 'Mary. We saw his face in the porridge, and then that happened. That is fucking spooky.'

'It is,' she said. 'But he's fine, thank God. Really, imagine he was on the motorway or somewhere, like, busy.'

Jason put his spoon down into his porridge and pushed the bowl away. 'I'm not touching it,' he said.

'Don't be silly,' she said, picking up her knife and fork to eat her own breakfast. She was having toast and poached eggs.

'I'm serious,' he said, folding his arms. 'I know it sounds daft, but do you expect me to put that porridge in my mouth after that?'

'You're right,' she said. 'It does sound daft. Eat your porridge.'

'Mary, we saw Charlie's face in the porridge, and there he goes and has an accident. And you expect me to put that in my mouth? C'mon, where are the Frosties? Have you put them somewhere?'

She ignored him.

He looked at his bowl as it sat halfway across the table towards Mary. He pulled it over to himself and looked inside. He looked to Mary, but she was busy with her own breakfast. He shook his head and got back to his porridge.

A few days passed.

Jason and Mary left messages on Deborah and Charlie's Facebook pages to wish them well. Deborah suggested that Jason should tell Charlie about the porridge thing, to give Charlie a laugh, but Jason said he'd rather not think any more about it. He said he was really struggling to eat the porridge, and he just wanted his Frosties. Mary always said no. She said there was no connection between what they saw in the porridge and what happened to Charlie, and Jason was to stop being so silly. He was to just stop.

So he did. He stopped complaining and going on about how spooky it all was. He even began to joke about it. Mary would sometimes ask him if he could see somebody else's face in the porridge, and she joked about how she hoped that he would pull out the face of her boss or her brother-in-law or somebody else she didn't like, and they'd both have a laugh about it.

While laughing, he asked her if he could have Frosties.

She said no. And that upset him.

He told her that he'd rather pull a face out of the porridge and for something terrible to happen than for nothing to happen. His preference, of course, would be to have Frosties and to not pull out any faces. But if he was forced to eat porridge, he'd rather pull out a face. That's how much it was getting to him. He couldn't go on eating this gruel. Mary told him to stop it. Just stop.

Then, one day, it happened again.

They hadn't talked about faces in the porridge for over a week. Jason had been quiet. Not one complaint. He put his spoon into the bowl, under the pool of soy milk at the top, and lifted out a lump of porridge.

And there, on the spoon, was another face.

Jason held it up in front of him, and waited for Mary to see. She was looking at her phone. When she sensed that Jason wasn't moving or making a sound, she looked up to see him sitting as still as a picture.

'What is it?' she asked. 'What you doing?'

He didn't reply. He just looked at the porridge. He looked scared.

'Jason,' she said. 'What are you doing?'

'Look,' he said, without taking his eyes off the spoon. 'Look at this.'

Mary stood up and walked around to his side of the table, and looked at the porridge. She looked for a while, but didn't see anything of interest. It didn't even look like a face, never mind one that she recognised.

'Who is it?' she whispered, while moving her hands around in a mystical manner. 'Who do you seeeee?' She was taking the piss.

Jason snapped out of it, and looked at her.

'Who d'you think that looks like?' he asked.

'I don't know,' she said. 'Are you saying it looks like somebody?'

'Can you not see?'

She looked again, as he turned the spoon in different ways.

'Hmmm,' she said. 'No.'

She began to walk away, but he stopped her when he said who he thought it looked like. 'Your dad.'

She looked at him and screwed up her face. She walked back towards him and had a look at the porridge on the spoon again.

It didn't look like her dad. 'It looks nothing like him,' she said.

'It does,' said Jason. 'No offence, but look. The wrinkles.'

He pointed at some of the creases between the lumps of oats.

'Oh Jason,' she laughed. 'You're clutching at straws now. Wrinkles? That could be anybody over 40. That could be me.'

'Not just the wrinkles,' he said. 'But you know that spot your dad's got at the side of his nose?'

She smiled and had a closer look at the porridge, but she couldn't see where he meant. He pointed it out with his pinky. One oat was poking out slightly more than the others.

'Jason,' she said.

He replied quickly with 'Can I please have Frosties?'

'Jason,' she said again. 'You're insane.'

'Am I?' he asked, as she walked back to her seat, but she didn't hear him.

She sat down and continued eating her breakfast. She picked up her phone to have a read of an article she was looking at. When she sensed that Jason was still watching her, she laughed and looked back.

He was very still and calm.

She said, 'You're giving me the creeps looking at me like that.'

He didn't say anything, then he blinked and said, 'Am I insane?'

She put down her phone and asked, 'What are you saying, Jason? You really think you're getting a premonition? In porridge? Is that really what you think?'

'I don't want to eat it, Mary. I really don't want to.'

'Jason,' she said.

'Please just get me the Frosties,' said Jason. 'Have you hidden them? Or did you bin them? I cannae eat this porridge, this isnae right.'

She looked at her phone and shook her head. 'You're insane, you really are.' She laughed, but it was a fake laugh.

A week passed. Then something happened.

Mary phoned Jason in the afternoon to tell him. 'Jason,' she said.

'Hello,' said Jason. 'What is it? I can't speak, I'm driving. What is it?'

She didn't answer, and he thought she'd been cut off. So he said 'Hello?' again.

'It's my dad,' said Mary. 'He's in hospital.'

Jason told her that he was pulling over the motor to talk to her.

When he got parked, he picked up his phone again and said, 'Mary. What? What is it? Did he fall or something?'

'Fall? No. It was they wee cunts.'

'What wee cunts?' he asked. 'What?'

She reminded Jason of the local youngsters her dad had been moaning about for a while.

Her dad lived in a ground-floor flat, which meant that if youngsters decided to stand about and yap away near his block, it would be as if they were yapping away right inside his own living room. He couldn't hear the telly.

Mary had always advised him to just let it pass, which he used to do, but recently he had taken to opening the window and having a word with them. Mary was worried that they'd make him a target, but he said he'd never get any backchat, they'd apologise and move on, they seemed harmless.

'But obviously not that harmless,' she said. 'The wee fucking bastards.'

'Mary, what happened?' asked Jason.

So she told him.

Earlier that day, her dad was watching *This Morning*. He had just made himself a cup of tea, and had picked it up from the table to drink it. Then a brick came flying through the window and hit him on the shoulder. His face was cut from the glass and he spilled the full cup of piping hot tea on his chest. A neighbour heard him shouting in pain, then knocked on the door, and an ambulance was phoned.

After Mary finished telling the story, Jason was quiet, and it was Mary's turn to wonder if they had been disconnected.

'Hello?' she said.

'Mary,' said Jason. 'The porridge.'

She told him to shut up.

The next morning, Mary made herself her breakfast. A bowl of Shredded Wheat, with a plate of pistachio nuts to the side. Then she made porridge as usual, and put it down on the table in front of Jason.

He couldn't believe it.

He had watched her make it without saying a word, and now he sat looking at it in the bowl, with the soy milk on top, as he sat there in silence.

She began eating, then looked at Jason, who wasn't eating. She shook her head and looked at her phone.

'Mary,' he said, quietly, looking into the porridge.

'No,' she said.

But he continued.

'First, I pull out Charlie's face, and he has an accident.'

'A coincidence,' she said, still looking at her phone.

'Then we saw your dad's face.'

'No,' she said. 'Not we. You. You saw my dad's face.'

'And I'm just worried,' said Jason. 'That one day I'm going to put my spoon into the porridge and pull out another face. And that face will be yours.'

She looked up from her phone when he said that. She wasn't sure what she was going to do, if she was going to laugh at him, or be angry at him for going on about seeing things in his porridge when her dad was in hospital.

But then she saw that he was crying.

'Jason,' she said. 'I don't know what's wrong with you, but there is no connection between the porridge and the things that have happened. I know it's spooky, but please stop it. My dad's in hospital.'

'I put the brick through your dad's window,' said Jason. 'It was me who did the thing to Charlie's brakes. I can't eat the porridge anymore, Mary, I'm serious. I don't know what's happening to me. I want my Frosties. Where are they? Have you hidden them?'

The Clown

It was Colin's first day as a clown. A children's clown. His first day on the job, officially.

He'd always wanted to be a clown, he had a knack for it. He was good at tricks, and he was good with weans. His sister had a couple of wee twins and they loved his magic tricks. He reckoned he could get a right good career out of it. He didn't want to be a circus clown, he preferred close-up magic, doing it right there in the living room. Plus he imagined that circus clowns don't get work as regular as children's clowns.

He looked up how to get into it, and met up with a few other folk who were clowns. They told him the job wasn't as easy as he might think, it isn't all fun and games. Some of them even seemed a bit miserable, a bit worn out. But he couldn't imagine ever getting like that. He was being a clown, after all. It was entertaining, it was unpredictable, and seeing the surprise on people's faces was almost payment in itself.

He put his details online, and it didn't take long for him to get a phone call, by a mum in Partick called Lesley.

She was having a birthday party for her five-year-old son Oliver, and she wanted to know what kind of things she could expect. Colin told her that he did jokes, card tricks, disappearing tricks, he pulled things out of his magic hat, he did balloon animals. She said all that sounded perfect. She asked him if he could be over there at 11 a.m. on the Saturday.

And with that, he had just got himself his first job. He told his clown mates the good news, and they wished him all the best, in their slightly jaded sort of way.

He drove to Lesley's flat in Partick, arriving five minutes early. He chapped on the door, holding his suitcase of tricks. He had a look at himself before the door was opened. He fixed his stripy trousers so they were sitting well on his colourful brogues. There was a piece of fluff on his red T-shirt just above his waist, and he brushed it off. He had a look in the mirrored nameplate on the door to check his nose. He'd painted it red, just the tip. He'd checked it in the mirror in the car before he came up, but he had another look anyway.

He wanted his first day to be perfect. And so far so good.

The door was answered by Lesley, who seemed rushed off her feet and happy to see him.

'Oh thank God,' she said. 'In you come.'

'Thanks,' said Colin, and he walked inside. He stopped when he remembered that he'd left his suitcase outside the front door, and he turned quickly to pick it up. He didn't want Lesley to see that mistake, and she didn't. But he thought that if she had seen it, he could have passed it off as part of the act. He knew that it was a mistake, though, and he hoped there weren't any more.

He walked into the hall with the suitcase, and he could hear the weans somewhere in the flat. It sounded like there were about 20 of them. Some of them ran through the hall, then stopped to look at him, then ran into the living room.

He felt nervous, but he tried not to show it.

'So,' said Lesley. 'How do you want to do it?'

He pointed to where he'd just seen the weans run, and asked if that was the living room. She said it was, and he said that he'd get set up in there then. He told her that if she could clear everybody out of there for a wee while, that would be great, he wouldn't be long.

'No bother,' she said, and she got everybody out.

After he was set up, he poked his head out the door and told Lesley that he was ready now to start the show.

'Kids!' she shouted. 'It's time for the clown!' She looked at him and whispered, 'What's your name again?'

'Coco,' he said. 'Coco the Clown.'

'Love it,' she said. Then she shouted again. 'Come on and see Coco the Clown!'

Colin went back into the living room and waited for the weans to come in. As they came in, they looked at him. Some were shy, some were excited.

'Sit down, sit down,' he said, owning the room. He was aiming to be confident, but not too loud and dominating. He wanted them to know he was a silly man, he wasn't their teacher or their mum and dad. 'The show's about to start,' he said. 'That's it, sit anywhere, on you go. My name's Coco. Coco the Clown. Sit anywhere.'

They sat on the floor. There were around 15 of them, boys and lassies, and some of the adults came in to watch as well, including Lesley and a guy who Colin assumed was her man, because they were leaning up against each other.

'Okay, kids,' he said. 'Hands up who likes magic.'

The hands all shot up, even the hands belonging to the shy weans.

'Well, I'm very glad to hear that. Because that's what I do. My name's Coco the Clown, and I do magic tricks. Who wants to see one right now?'

The hands went up again, and some started saying 'Me, me!'

Lesley smiled at Mark, her man, who was smiling as well. This clown seemed good, he thought. He wasn't one of the scary ones with the bald head and the colourful hair around the side, he was just a normal cunt being a clown. A modern kind of clown. Mark liked it.

'All right,' said Colin to the weans, walking in amongst them. 'I'll do a show, but first you've got to pay me. I don't work for free, Mum and Dad!'

The grown-ups laughed. A bit of patter for the grown-ups there.

'Now, who's got the money?' said Colin, looking at each of the weans. And then 'Ah! There it is!' And he leaned down to pull a 50-pence piece from behind the ear of a wee lassie.

The weans went 'Ahhhhh!' at the clown pulling a coin out from nowhere. The wee lassie smiled and checked behind her ear with her hand to see if there were any more coins.

A wee boy said, 'I know how it's done, I know, I know!'

'Ah ah ah,' said Colin, wagging his finger and smiling. 'Don't ruin the magic. Otherwise I'd be out of a job. Isn't that right, mums and dads?'

Another bit of patter for the grown-ups. The guy was good. He had something for everybody.

And on he continued, doing various tricks for the weans, like pulling things out of his magic bowler hat, or guessing what card the wean was holding.

He'd sometimes pretend to make a mistake, like guessing the wrong card, to give the weans a laugh and make the adults think he was making an arse of it. But then they'd realise that it was just part of a bigger trick, when he'd say, 'Oh, I forgot what card you had, but it's all right, I had it written down', then he got Oliver to take off his shoe, and there in the shoe was a piece of paper with the four of hearts written on it.

'Now, that was good,' said Mark, and Lesley agreed. Money well spent, so this was. The clown charged £100 an hour. It seemed a lot when she booked it, and she had to get the other parents to chip in. But 100 quid to keep a room full of weans entertained for an hour solid. Only a parent would know that was money well spent.

She checked the time, and saw that there were five minutes left. Colin saw her looking, and it reminded him that it was time to wrap things up.

'Okay, kids,' he said. 'It's time for me to go.'

'Awwww,' they all said, including the grown-ups.

Colin pretended to have a think to himself, then he smiled. 'Would you like one more trick?'

'Yeeeah!' shouted the weans.

'All right,' said Colin, looking into his suitcase. 'Now, where is it? Ah, there it is.'

He reached into his suitcase and pulled out a sheet. A dark purple, velvety sheet covered in stars. 'Here it is,' he said. 'Now, I need a volunteer. Someone who is very brave. A very brave boy, I wonder if there's one here.'

He turned towards Lesley and said, 'Can you think of one, Mum?'

She understood. 'Oh, I can think of one.' She didn't want to make the other boys and girls jealous, so she said, 'There are lots of brave boys here. And girls! But I know one in particular whose birthday it is.'

'Yeeeah!' said Oliver, sticking up his hand.

'Then up you come, brave Oliver!' said Colin. 'Give him a big round of applause.'

They all clapped, as Oliver stood up and walked to the clown.

'Now, Oliver,' said Colin. 'Have you ever wanted to disappear?'

'Yes!' said Oliver.

'Has your mummy or daddy ever got you into trouble, and you wished you could just vanish into thin air?'

'Yes!' he said.

'Oh, I bet,' said Lesley.

'And what about you, Mummy and Daddy?' asked Colin, smiling. 'Has Oliver ever been a tiny bit naughty and you wished that he disappeared?'

Lesley said 'Oh yes', and they all smiled and laughed.

'I can see that some of the other mummies and daddies are thinking the same thing,' said Colin, and they all laughed again.

Colin was pleased with the reaction. He'd rehearsed what he said to Oliver, but he was ad-libbing when he talked to the parents. He took a mental note to write some of that patter into the act next time.

'All right,' he said. 'I'll see what I can do. Come, Oliver, you stand right there. And then I'll just do this.'

Colin held up the purple, sparkly sheet so that it hid Oliver from view from the rest of the room.

'Are you ready to vanish, Oliver?' asked Colin.

'Yeah!' said Oliver.

'All right. Then get ready. One, two, three. Shazam!'

Colin whipped away the sheet, and Oliver was gone.

The room gasped.

The weans were amazed, and sat with their mouths open and eyes smiling. But the adults were dumb-founded, their brains working overtime to figure out how the fuck he did that.

Mark had an idea of how it was done. What he reck-oned was that when the sheet had been held up, Oliver had crawled behind the seat next to the clown, and when the clown saw that Oliver was in the clear, he whipped the sheet away to make it look like he'd vanished. And in a minute, the clown would hold the sheet up again, and Oliver will crawl back and reappear. Mark had done the same thing himself with Oliver a year or two ago with a quilt.

'Okay everyone,' said Colin. 'Byyye!' and he closed his suitcase and walked out the living-room door, which made the grown-ups laugh. The weans just shouted bye.

Lesley waited for the clown to come back in, but he didn't. So it looked like that was the end of the routine. She shrugged at Mark and walked out to the hall, where the clown was waiting.

'Oh that was great,' said Lesley, going into her pocket for the money. 'Fantastic show. Money well spent.'

'Thank you very much,' said Colin, pleased with how it went himself. He'd made a wee mistake with one of the card tricks at the beginning, but he didn't think anybody noticed. Other than that, it couldn't have gone better.

'Ah, but what have you done with my boy?' she said, smiling, bringing the money close to her chest. She looked into the living room. She saw Mark looking behind the seat. She had the same idea about how the trick was done.

She saw Mark then tipping the seat back and looking under it. He got down on his knees and tapped around at the black fabric underneath, presumably feeling around for Oliver.

Then he looked behind the seat again. Then he looked around the room.

He saw Lesley watching him, then he looked behind the seat again. He looked at Lesley and shrugged, then pointed to the clown, to suggest that she should have a word with him.

She stopped smiling, and looked at Colin.

'Where is he really?' she asked.

'He's vanished,' said Colin, smiling. 'Shazam!'

He put his hand out for the money, but she wasn't giving it over. Not yet.

'No, seriously,' she asked. 'Where did he go? I know he didn't vanish, but I need to know where he is, in case he sneaked out the door.'

The clown didn't answer. He looked confused. Lesley turned away from the living room and towards the kitchen door. 'Mum!' she shouted.

'Aye?' came an older voice. And out walked Lesley's mum from the kitchen. 'What?'

'Is Oliver back there?' asked Lesley.

'Oliver? No. I don't think so. Wait there.' She walked back into the kitchen.

Lesley looked at Colin again. 'Mate, where is he?'

Mark came walking out of the living room, with a couple of the other parents behind him. They all looked concerned. 'Lesley,' he said. 'I cannae find him. Mate, where is he?'

One of the other parents said something about how everything will be fine.

Colin didn't know what was going on here. 'I don't know what you mean,' he said, looking at them all.

Lesley and Mark raised their voices, talking over each other.

'What d'you mean you don't know what we mean?' asked Lesley.

'Where's my son, mate?' asked Mark.

'Where is he?' asked Lesley.

The parent who said that everything will be fine was telling them to calm down a bit, but he agreed that the joke had gone far enough.

Colin looked at Lesley and Mark. 'He's gone. You saw.'

He looked to the parent that had been appealing for Lesley and Mark to stay calm, hoping that maybe the guy would help explain, even though there was nothing to explain. But they all looked back with the same unhappy expression.

This was getting scary.

'Gone where?' shouted Lesley, giving Colin a fright.

Mark put his hand on her shoulder. They all listened for the answer. Lesley's mum came back from the kitchen and said, 'No, he's not back there.' When she saw the body language and faces of everybody outside the living room, she asked, 'What's happened?' But nobody turned towards her. All eyes were on Colin.

He didn't know what else to tell them. How else could he put it? They saw what happened.

Mark stepped forward to grab him. Like the other parent said, the joke had gone far enough.

Colin didn't know if Mark intended to hurt him, but he didn't want to take any chances, because it was all beginning to turn into a mob. There was an insanity taking over the group, and he wanted to get out of there, and get out of there now.

He reached into his pocket, and threw a ball on the ground. A small explosion threw up a swirl of red smoke. Lesley's mum said 'Oh!' and stood back.

Mark reached into the smoke to grab the cunt, but there was nothing there. He kept walking with his arms outstretched, but all he felt was the wall at the other side of the hall.

When the smoke drifted away, they saw that the clown was gone.

The following Monday, Colin told his fellow clowns all about it. He told them about how everything had been going so well. He told them that the kids loved the show, he told them that the adults liked the wee ad-libs he was throwing in and that he planned to write them down for next time. He told them that it couldn't have went any better. Yet, at the end, all the parents started acting mental. An insane mob. Torches and pitchforks stuff. And for the life of him, he just couldn't understand why.

The other clowns nodded, knowingly. All too knowingly.

Colin didn't understand.

He asked them if they thought he'd be able to get the money he was owed. That 100 quid. It was a full hour that he did, and the parents seemed happy with the show, until the very end. Until after the very end, in fact.

'You can forget it,' grumbled Bobo from the back.

Bobo was the oldest of the clowns.

He had a red nose, but not because it was painted or stuck on. It was because of the whisky. The only fucking thing that got you through this job.

Biscuits

Listen to this.

Try and work this out.

I've got this mate, and I went over to his flat one night to play some *FIFA* and have a drink. We're always playing *FIFA*. He's shite at it and he's always trying to beat me, but he never does. He sometimes does, but very, very rarely.

Anyway, I was going through a bit of a fat phase at the time, so I ate pretty much all his biscuits. And he had a lot of biscuits. A lot.

This is top secret, by the way. Not the thing about eating his biscuits, I mean what I'm about to tell you. Utterly top secret.

I ate tons of his biscuits. He has this biscuit jar, which is a bit unusual for a single guy. A biscuit jar. It's something you'd expect maybe an older couple to have or an old granny. But he has one, and that goes to show you that he likes his biscuits. There's a reason for me pointing that out. I just want you to know that he eats the biscuits in his biscuit jar, they're not just for visitors. He disnae just buy them for me.

So I ate pretty much all of his biscuits in this biscuit jar. He had lots of different types. Good ones, cheap ones. Cheap ones like custard creams and wafers, good ones like Fox's Classic and Choco Leibniz. I pretty much finished the lot of them while we were playing *FIFA*, probably about a tenner's worth, and he was like that to me: 'Fuck sake.'

The jar was up to the top with biscuits before, and now it was almost down to the bottom. Right? Remember that.

A few days later, I head back up to his for a rematch at *FIFA*. That's what he always calls it: a rematch. It's a bit daft, because 'rematch' sort of implies that it's a decider, like it could go either way. But I'm winning all the time.

Anyway, on the way there, I thought it would be good to pop into the shops and get some new biscuits for him. I grabbed a packet of this and a packet of that. I cannae remember what I got, but it was a mix of cheap one and fancy ones, a bit like what he had in the jar.

So I took the biscuits up to his. But you know what I thought would be funny?

BISCUITS

If I filled up his biscuit jar, but didnae tell him.

I thought it would be funny if I filled it up without telling him, and if he was to ask me 'Did you fill that up?' I'd say no. Like it just filled up by itself.

I knew he'd work out it was me, because nobody else ever went up to his. He didnae even get his family over. But I thought it would be funny for a few minutes, just a wee joke.

So when I got into his, he got things started with the PlayStation in the living room, and I went into his kitchen to get a drink. And then I took the biscuits out of my pockets and filled up the jar.

I never told him that I was gonnae do that, he didnae know it was happening.

Anyway, I went through to the living room, and we played *FIFA* for a bit. I didnae take the jar through. But after a while, I said to him, 'Can I have some biscuits?'

And he said, 'Aye, if there's any left!'

He knew the biscuits were almost finished, right?

And I went into the kitchen and brought back the jar, the jar that I had filled with biscuits without telling him, and I started pulling out biscuits and munching them. Biscuits that I bought.

He didnae notice, though. So I said, 'See? There's plenty.'

But he just said, 'Ah, right. Good,' and kept on playing.

So even though he knew that there were hardly any left before, and he knew that he hidnae bought any new ones himself, suddenly there are these new biscuits filling the jar right up to the top, and he didnae think that was anything out of the ordinary.

I asked him if anybody had been up to his flat since the last time I was there. I didnae say I was asking because of the biscuits, I told him I was just wondering. But what I was really asking for was to find out if maybe somebody visited and brought biscuits. But he said nobody had come. Nobody ever went up to his flat, it was always just me.

Yet somehow these biscuits had appeared and he didnae notice. Mental. He's the sort of person that notices things, by the way, he's not a dope. That's what was so mental about it.

Then I left, without saying anything about the biscuits. I was waiting for him to say something about it just before I left, like 'Nice try winding me up, by the way'. But he didnae.

And during the week, I was waiting for him to give me a text saying that he'd just noticed that biscuits had magically appeared in the jar after I turned up. Sometimes it takes a bit of time for you to notice something, for it to click. I was waiting for that moment during the week.

But no. Nothing.

I went up to his about a week later, up for another game and a drink, and I sneaked in some more biscuits. I reckoned he'd probably munched a few himself after I left the time before. So I was gonnae top up the jar again, to see if he'd notice the second time around.

I went into his kitchen to look at the biscuit jar, and I could see that I was right about him munching a few. When I left the time before, I'd eaten the biscuits to about halfway down the jar. Since then, he'd almost finished the rest, there were just a few left. I'm talking about two or three biscuits at the most.

I filled it up again. I filled it right to the top. It was even more obvious than before, I think. But this time, I didnae take the jar through to the living room. I thought I'd just leave it like that, full up to the top. That way, he'd look at the jar, and see it full, which would look completely different from the last time he saw it, which was almost empty. I cannae really explain my thinking, but I thought that would make it more obvious.

Anyway, I leave at the end of the night, having said nothing about the biscuits. Neither of us mentioned them.

And I come back a few days later, up for another game, and about half the biscuits have been eaten. He's eaten half the jar of biscuits. Biscuits that he didnae have before.

And he disnae say a thing about it.

I asked him if anybody had been up since the last time I was up, just pretending I was making conversation, and he said there hidnae been.

Think about that.

He knows that the biscuit jar is empty.

Then it's suddenly full of biscuits.

And it's only him that's eating the biscuits now, it isnae somebody else. I don't touch them. I don't bring the jar through to the living room.

He's eating the biscuits until the jar is almost empty, then it gets full again, without explanation. And he's saying nothing.

You'd think he'd have said something. You'd think he would have said, 'Here, the strangest fucking thing is happening to me right now. It's that biscuit jar, you willnae believe it.'

But he's said nothing.

I really don't understand that. I cannae get it out of my head.

It's all I think about when we're playing *FIFA*.

And he's been whipping me.

Absolutely whipping me.

Suzie Spunkstain

Davie was getting married. He was waiting at the altar, waiting for his bride to show up. Her name was Suzie Milligan. But to some of the other people here, she was known by another name.

Suzie Spunkstain.

He didn't know that, he'd only just found out. He'd only just heard about it the night before, at the stag do. He'd known her for over three years, but that was the first time he'd heard the nickname. He learned that she got it when she was younger, where she grew up, here in Manchester. And he wasn't from here.

He'd moved down for a job, and it was in work that he met Suzie. She was from Manchester herself. They got on right away, going out for a drink together on the same week that he joined the company. There was nothing sexual in it to begin with, not in a way that they'd admit to anyway. It was just a friendly gesture. Suzie asked Davie if he fancied coming out for a drink after work, and the pair of them thought that more people from their office would come along, but it ended up just being the two of them.

And one thing led to another.

Now here he was at the altar, waiting for Suzie. Suzie Milligan, soon to be Suzie McIver.

Suzie Spunkstain.

He couldn't stop thinking about it. It had been stuck in his head since last night, when he first got told.

He'd brought down a load of his mates from Glasgow, and they all teamed up with a load of his new mates from down in Manchester, including a few mates of Suzie's brother Stuart, who was also there. They'd all got steaming. Stuart's mate Harvey was in a particularly bad way, talking mumbo jumbo to himself and winding people up.

He spoke to Davie in one of the pub toilets.

'Suzie Spunkstain,' Harvey had said, while pishing into the urinal next to Davie.

He hadn't said it very loud, he hadn't directed it at Davie to start a fight. He'd just said it while looking into the bowl.

'What was that?' asked Davie.

Harvey told him that he didn't mean anything by it. He pulled up his zip and tried to leave, but Davie wouldn't let him. He'd had enough of Harvey that night.

'What did you say?' asked Davie. 'You said Suzie. Suzie something. Suzie what?'

So Harvey told him.

He said that Suzie's nickname was Suzie Spunkstain. She got it when they were all younger, when they were teenagers. That's all. 'That's her nickname,' said Harvey, as he looked between Davie and the door. 'Don't blame me, that's her nickname. Everybody says it.'

Davie wanted to know why. But in a way, he didn't need to know. He already knew why. He knew about nicknames like that.

He once knew a lassie when he was younger. It was a lassie that he liked, but he never went near her, because of the nickname she'd been given.

Quickfuck. That's what they called her. Quickfuck.

He used to ask people why she was called that, but nobody knew for certain. He got two different answers: one was that she shagged quickly, like a rabbit; the other was that you could get a quick shag off her any time you wanted.

Whatever the reason for the name, he knew the reason why she was given it. It was to shame her. It was to bring shame upon her, and anybody who went near her.

And it worked.

Despite liking her, he just couldn't get past that name.

She knew he liked her, and she liked him as well, so she could never understand why he never wanted to be with her, alone. If the two of them were left alone, he'd always be asking where everybody was and he'd be wanting to find them, or he'd simply avoid being left alone with her in the first place. She once asked him to walk her home through the park one night, because it was too dodgy to walk through herself. But he said no. He let her walk by herself, a 14-year-old lassie, a lassie less than half the age he was now, because of that nickname.

He didn't tell her why. And she couldn't guess why either, because she didn't know. She never knew about her nickname. She couldn't say, 'Are you treating me like shit because of that fucking nickname?' Because she never knew.

He'd lost out. She'd lost out. And it wasn't because of her, it was because of him. That was the shame. The shame was on him, and it stuck like shite.

He was only young at the time, he could almost forgive himself. Yet here he was doing it again. When Harvey told him Suzie's nickname, he did it again. He would have expected himself to not care. But he did. There was still a part of him, a teenage part, that still cared about all that. If he didn't care, he would have let

Harvey go or he would have walked out of there himself. But he didn't.

Instead, he asked, 'What was she called that for?' He tried to look happy, not ashamed, like he was nothing more than curious. But he wasn't just curious. There was that part of him, that teenage part, that wanted to gauge how much he should be ashamed. Ashamed of her. He wanted to know how much had she shamed herself on a scale of 1 to 10.

Harvey told him where the name came from.

She used to go out with some guy when they were young. At the weekends they'd hang about the school at night, when it was shut. She walked away with her boyfriend on one of these nights, over to the shelters, then she came back later with him, hand in hand.

One of the crowd pointed at her leggings and shouted, 'Look! A spunkstain!'

And that was her from then on.

Suzie Spunkstain.

Davie laughed, like it did not bother him one bit, like he was looking forward to laughing about it with Suzie herself. He patted Harvey on the back as Harvey left the toilet, but Davie stayed inside. Then he walked to the cubicle and sat inside to think about it.

His wife to be was Suzie Spunkstain.

Suzie Spunkstain.

So?

Well, he would just like to have known, that's all. He wouldn't have minded. He'd just like to have known. But she didn't tell him, now he was hearing it from this Harvey cunt.

And?

So?

So fucking what?

The voice inside his head was right. So what?

He stood at the altar and thought of last night, why he let it get to him, it wasn't like him. He was drunk, that was it. Last night, he was drunk. That's why it got into his head, because when a person is drunk, it can make them childish. It can make them think like a child.

But he was an adult now. A grown up. Here at an altar, waiting to be married. Waiting for her.

Waiting for Suzie Spunkstain.

It was funny. That was a good way to look at it. It was funny.

He'd joke about it later. He'd show her he didn't care. Of course he didn't care, he was a grown man, we've all got histories. He'd tell her he found out, and that he just laughed when he heard. And that would be it. That would put it to rest.

It would perhaps even put things to rest with Quickfuck.

He thought about her, about Quickfuck, or whatever her real name was. He hoped that she was somewhere in the world, happy. Happy in herself. He wondered if she ever found out about her nickname, and he hoped that she laughed it off. Maybe she had a daughter, and told her daughter all about it, and how none of that shite matters. Fuck them.

He hoped she was happy. As happy as he would make Suzie.

He looked back towards the front door of the church. Suzie's brother Stuart was walking swiftly up the aisle towards Davie. He was smiling at the guests, but it wasn't a relaxed smile. It wasn't a happy-go-lucky smile. It was a reassuring smile, where you're trying to tell everybody that everything's fine, despite it not really being fine.

Stuart told Davie the news.

Davie looked to his family in the seats. They looked back at him with questioning looks on their faces.

He shook his head.

His mum knew something was wrong, her boy looked heartbroken.

Davie asked Stuart if it was a joke. If it was a joke, he wanted to know now, because he could see that it was upsetting his mum.

But it wasn't a joke. Suzie had called the wedding off.

Davie asked Stuart why, if he knew the reason why, if she said why. But Stuart didn't know. He really didn't, Suzie wouldn't tell him.

She was ashamed to tell him.

She'd found out last night, at the hen night. She'd found out from one of Davie's sister's pals, Anne. Anne told Suzie she was so happy for Davie, so happy that he'd found somebody, because it had been so hard for him up in Glasgow.

Because of, well, you know.

But Suzie didn't know.

And when she found out, she knew she couldn't go ahead. She was sorry, she loved the guy, but there was just no way she could marry Davie.

Davie McIver.

The Moggy Muff Diver.

He Licked Oot a Cat for the Price of a Fiver.

The Curtain

Iain had bought a curtain, for his and Maggie's bedroom. He thought it was just a normal curtain, but it wasn't. It was alive. It would wake them up during the night, and batter fuck out of them.

Maggie told him she wanted it out the house, but he told her that the curtain was probably behaving that way because it was in a new house, with new owners. It was probably something like that. It would settle down eventually.

She said she'd never heard anything so stupid in her life. When had you ever heard of anybody having a problem like that with any other curtain? When had they themselves ever had any problems like that with curtains in the past?

Iain told her that it obviously wasn't like any other curtain. She told him that she didn't need convincing when it came to that. It certainly wasn't like any other curtain, she agreed with him there.

'Just give it a chance to settle in,' he said.

'No, Iain.'

'Please,' he said. 'It cost a lot of money.'

'Well,' said Maggie. 'That's your problem.'

'Well,' said Iain, 'it's not really.' And he reminded her that they had a joint bank account.

'You are a fucking idiot for getting that curtain,' she said. 'You really are.'

But he asked her again to please give the curtain a chance. One more chance. Please, just one more chance.

She thought about it, and said yes.

They didn't know if the curtain had been listening to the conversation, listening to how it was on its last chance, but for the next few days Iain and Maggie had a good night's sleep with no disturbances.

Maggie had trouble nodding off for the first few nights, thinking at the back of her mind that she was going to get attacked the second she closed her eyes. But then she relaxed and told herself that everything was all right now.

Then, on Wednesday, in the middle of the night, she got woken up to the curtain whipping her face.

It was floating in the air and whipping her in the same way that boys in changing rooms whip each other with towels. Wa-*disssssh*. It looked like it was having a right old time.

Maggie slapped Iain across the cheek. She didn't bother shouting his name, she was well past that point. She slapped him hard, again and again, until he woke up and saw what was happening.

'Oh fuck, no,' he mumbled. Then he stood up, still half asleep, and tried to grab the thing.

It flew out the way and wrapped itself around Maggie's throat, then yanked her up from the bed.

Iain jumped on both of them and wrestled the curtain away, until he and the curtain fell off the bed and the curtain stopped moving.

Maggie looked at the time. It was 2.32 a.m.

'Right,' she said, rubbing her throat. 'I want that curtain out of here. I want it out of this house right fucking now.'

'No,' he said. 'Look. Listen.'

'Right now, Iain,' she said. 'Right fucking now. Right fucking *now*!'

She was shouting.

'Right, right,' he said, and carried the curtain out of the room.

A while later, he came back without the curtain. She shook her head at him and turned off the light.

A few days passed. It was a few lovely nights of unin-terrupted sleep. A few days without that curtain.

Then, one morning, Maggie walked into the living room with her breakfast to watch the telly, and there was the curtain hanging up in the living-room window.

She nearly dropped her bowl.

'Iain!' she shouted. 'What the fuck is this? Iain!'

Iain started talking before he walked into the room. 'Right, listen. Listen, right?'

'I thought you got fucking rid of it,' she said.

'Listen, right?'

'Don't want to hear it, Iain,' she said, having a spoonful of Alpen, shaking her head. 'Hmm-hmm. No. Want it out. Now.'

He asked her to listen. Just listen. The curtain would never be going back into the bedroom, she didn't have to worry about that. That was an absolute guarantee, that was a promise. But he didn't want to just chuck out a 400-quid curtain.

Maggie spat out some of her Alpen. 'Four fucking …'

He told her that maybe the curtain was just in the wrong room, that's all. Maybe it wasn't meant for the bedroom, maybe it was meant for the living room. It suited the living room better, he thought, and asked her if she agreed.

'Four hundred fucking quid,' she said. 'Is that what you said?'

'Aye. But it's nice, you've got to admit it's nice.'

THE CURTAIN

'Four hundred quid, for a curtain?' she said, looking at it. It did look nice. It was a nice curtain. 'What the fuck were you thinking, Iain?'

'Is it nice?' he asked. 'It is nice, though.'

And it was nice. It was white and spotless. It was smooth and silky, and thick. It looked like when you see adverts for milk chocolate or cheese slices, and they show a jug of milk somehow being poured into the chocolate or cheese slice, to tell you how much milk is in it.

It was beautiful.

'But it isnae worth 400 fucking quid,' she said. 'And that's just for one. It's only one curtain. What the fuck were you thinking, just buying one curtain? I've only just realised that.'

'I know 400 is a lot,' he said. 'But it was reduced from 899. And I got it for 400. In fact, I got it for less than 400. It was 399.'

She considered the bargain, but there was a bigger fucking issue than that. 'Iain, it tried to kill me.'

'I disagree,' he said, sitting down on the armrest of the couch. 'I disagree. I don't think it was trying to kill you, but there's no doubt that what it did was wrong.' He looked at the curtain. 'But please, Maggie, just give it one more chance. Just give it a chance in here, in the living room.' He glided his hand around the room and said, 'I think it's a living-room curtain'.

Maggie looked at him, then looked at the curtain, and back to him. Then she walked out with her cereal.

A few days passed without any issues. Maggie continued to get her full eight hours of uninterrupted sleep in the bedroom. When they spent time in the living room, the curtain didn't cause any grief. It looked like it was a living-room curtain after all.

Then one night, it went for them.

They were watching *Masterchef*, and it went for them. Iain wrestled it to the ground again, until it stopped.

'I want it out,' said Maggie. 'And I fucking mean it, Iain. I want it out.'

'Maggie,' he said. 'It cost 400 fucking quid, I'm not going to just chuck it out. You don't just chuck out something that costs 400 fucking quid.'

'Then give it away,' she said. 'Or take it back. Or sell it. I don't fucking care, but whatever you do, I want it out now.' She pointed to the living-room door. 'Now, Iain. Right out the house.'

He couldn't take it back. He thought about it after the first attack in the bedroom. He tried taking it back to where he bought it, that wee shop that was down that lane. But when he walked down there, the shop was gone. It was like there never was a shop. He reckoned he must have went down the wrong lane, but it didn't matter. The fact was that he couldn't take it back.

Iain walked out the living room, carrying the curtain. And then he came back later without it.

'Is it out?' she asked.

'Aye,' he said.

'Where is it?'

'It disnae matter where it is.'

'Where is it? Is it in the house?'

'No,' he said. 'It's in the bin, all right?'

'The outside bin?'

'Aye,' he said.

He sat down to watch the rest of *Masterchef*, and saw that she hadn't paused it for him.

'Gonnae rewind it?' he asked.

'No.'

A couple of weeks passed, and it was good. A good night's sleep every night, and no interruptions to the telly.

Then, one night, they got a couple of pals over for something to eat. Their pals Michael and Leanne.

Iain told Maggie to put her feet up in the living room and he'd take care of the food. He'd give them all a shout when they could come through to the kitchen.

Maggie sat in the living room with Michael and Leanne, catching up. Leanne said the living room was looking nice, and Maggie was about to mention the episode with the curtain, but she decided not to.

After a while, Maggie came through to the kitchen to see how things were going and to see if Iain needed a hand. She saw that he had laid the table with four plates and a basket of bread in the middle, it was looking good.

'Oooh,' she said.

Under the plates and basket of bread was a tablecloth she hadn't seen before. A white tablecloth.

'Wait a minute,' she said. 'Is that that fucking curtain?'

'Keep your voice down,' he said, placing the knives and forks next to the plates.

'I asked you a question. Is that that fucking curtain?'

'Aye,' he said. He was trying to act calm like it was no big deal – he was going to stand his ground with this one. He carried on laying the cutlery on the table like this was going to happen whether she liked it or not.

She pointed at him. 'You said you binned it.'

'Look, I'm not binning a 400 quid curtain.'

'You're a fucking liar, Iain. You said you binned it.'

He stopped and waved his arms at the curtain on the table as it lay there peacefully. 'Look at it, Maggie. It's fine, all right? I tried it the other day when you were out.'

'I want it out,' she said. 'Get rid of it right fucking now, Iain. We've got people over.'

'No, Maggie. I tried it the other day, and it was fine. I don't even think it's a curtain. I think that's what the problem was. It isn't a curtain. It's a tablecloth.'

Michael and Leanne walked through from the living room. 'What are you two bickering about?' said Leanne. She looked at the table and said, 'Oh, very nice, very fancy. Nice tablecloth.' And she gave it a stroke.

Maggie nearly stepped forward to snatch away Leanne's arm, but Iain raised a hand to ask her to wait. And when nothing went wrong, Iain gave Maggie a smile that said, 'See? Everything's fine.'

They all sat down and had dinner.

Maggie wasn't sure. She was tense all throughout the first course. All throughout the soup. Waiting for something to happen.

By the time she was halfway into the main course, she had fully relaxed. Maybe Iain was right, and it was a tablecloth after all.

Then they all had dessert. Iain had made them all cranachan. Everybody said it was like something you'd get in a restaurant, except better, because there was more whisky.

'Is there enough cranachan in my whisky?' laughed Michael.

They sat around chatting for a while. Leanne and Maggie chatted about somebody they knew, and Iain and Michael chatted about Tom Middleton and what they thought about him.

Then, all of a sudden, the tablecloth went ballistic. Something set it off. It jerked around and flapped, pulling the table with it, buckarooing the bowls and plates and glasses and knives and forks in every direction, like a rodeo bull.

Leanne screamed as she was hit on her cheekbone with a fork. It almost went right in her eye.

Michael was banged on the chin with the table as it flew in the air, causing him to bite his tongue.

'Owwww, fuck!' he said, crouching away and heading for the door. 'I bit my fucking tongue.'

They all headed for the door, then slammed it behind them. They could hear the sound of everything in the kitchen being smashed to pieces.

Maggie hit Iain over the head with the palm of her hand. 'You fucking …'

She turned away, then turned back to hit him again and again, until Leanne had to stop her.

'Maggie, stop!' she said, grabbing Maggie's wrist.

Maggie stormed away into the living room, and Leanne followed. Michael followed Leanne. He turned around just before going into the living room to look at Iain, to say sorry for leaving him alone in the hall, but he had to go with Leanne.

The living-room door was kicked shut, hard. Iain

could hear them talking and he wanted to know what they were saying, but he could barely hear a word over the sound of the wreckage in the kitchen.

Maggie shouted, he could hear that. He heard her shout 'That guy!'

Iain couldn't see her from out in the hall, but he could hear from her voice that she was starting to cry.

'That fucking guy! Fucking idiot!'

He felt bad. He felt really, really bad. He knew he'd fucked up, big time, with that curtain.

But he didn't want to throw it out. It cost him 400 quid. Down from 899.

He didn't know what she was telling them in there, but you don't just chuck out a 400 quid curtain, especially when it's worth more than twice that.

In My Bin

I'm sitting in a bin.

I'm not doing it for a dare. There isn't anybody around that I'm showing off to. I haven't woken up here after a night on the piss. This isn't something I'm going to tell everybody about later and they'll all pat me on the back and tell me I'm a legend.

It's quite sad, actually, I think.

This bin I'm in, it's my bin. It's my wheelie bin. I'm in my wheelie bin, in the bin area for my block, around the back. It's two in the morning, I'm freezing, and I'm crouched down in my bin with the lid shut.

I'm standing up a bit now, and pushing the lid open and having a look out. I'm looking up to the back of the building, the back of the tenement building that I live in. I'm looking at flat 3/1, where I live. And now I'm looking below my flat, at flat 2/1, where Nick

THAT'S YOUR LOT

stays. Nick's probably all wrapped up in bed right now, all cosy.

I'm thinking about just getting out. Maybe I should just get out and go upstairs and get back into my bed as well. Maybe have a shower to get rid of the smell, then get into my bed and get all cosy.

But when I think about it, I know that if I do that then I'll just be right back to square one. Nothing will change. So I'm crouching back down and shutting the lid and I'm just going to sit here.

Part of me wants to get out again, to just open the lid and get out, because this is madness.

Or is it?

I've got every right to be here. Wouldn't you agree? I've got every right to be here, because it's my bin. I should remind myself of that.

And that's what this is all about: the fact that it's my bin. *Mine.* This is all about how it's my bin. And it's about Nick from downstairs.

Let me tell you about Nick.

He moved in about three months ago. The whole thing actually goes back further than that, about two years, just after I moved in myself. But what's brought things to this, to me being in this bin, is Nick.

Three months ago, I noticed the downstairs neighbours were moving out. Students. I was glad to see them go. There had been some hassle with them a

124

while back, some hassle regarding them putting stuff in my bin, but it was looking like things had been sorted out. I was always a wee bit on edge, though, that it would start up again. So I was glad to see the 'For Sale' sign go up.

And then, a while later, in moves this Nick. He moves in with his son, a wee boy. I don't know what age the boy is, I'm not good at knowing ages. I can tell you that he's at the age where you're old enough to walk but you're still wearing nappies. And I know that Nick's son wears nappies because there were nappies in my bin.

In my bin.

There were used nappies in my bin, and nobody else in the block wears nappies.

I thought that maybe it would be all right. Maybe Nick would be the sort of person I could talk to. It would be a fresh start, with somebody new. The thing with the students downstairs was that they had been there before I moved in, and I didn't feel confident enough to go up to people who were there before I was. Mind you, me and the students had been living in the block for so long that it didn't matter who had moved in first, so that wasn't the only reason. The main reason is probably that you just get used to it. You know how it is, if you don't say something in time. The longer you leave it, the harder it gets.

But I thought that maybe with this new guy down-stairs, there would be a new way of going about it. It wouldn't be that big a deal to say something. Maybe Nick would be a warm type of person, who might even say something first.

That's not how it was, though.

A few days after Nick moved in, I bumped into him on the stairs. I said hello and introduced myself, and Nick told me his name. I told him that I stayed in the flat upstairs, and I was smiling and apologising in advance for the sound of me walking about on the floorboards. I wasn't being serious. I was being half serious, because you can't help making a bit of noise if you stay upstairs. Everybody knows that. So that should have been Nick's cue to go, 'Oh, don't worry about it, mate.'

But Nick wasn't like that. Nick just said, 'Aye, well I hope there isnae any thumping about, I don't want my son getting woke up.'

He didn't say it in a threatening way, he didn't come right up to me, forehead to forehead. But he was seri-ous. There was no humour in it at all.

And d'you know what I did?

I said sorry.

I didn't say sorry for any thumping I'd already done, because I knew I hadn't done any, I always take my shoes off when I get in the flat. I walk about in my socks, so that I don't make a noise. I must be the only person in the block who does that. Even when I knew the students had moved out from downstairs and the flat was empty, I still made sure I took my shoes off when I got in, just out of habit. So there I was, apologising for something that hadn't happened, and something I wouldn't be doing in the future. I know I said I apologised in advance, but I said the second apology like I had actually done something wrong. I'm pathetic.

That's the type of guy I am. And why I'm in this bin. This bin that smells of Nick's son's nappies. Even though the bin's empty, except for me, there's still the smell of Nick's son's nappies. The bags must have burst at some point in the past. Bags that were never supposed to be here.

This is my bin.

I thought it had stopped with the students, but then it started up again with Nick.

About a week after Nick moved in, I came down here to the bin area with a bag. The bin area's at the rear of the back garden, and there are seven bins. There are seven green wheelie bins, one for each of the eight flats, but with one missing. And that had caused a bit of hassle in the past. In the past, nobody had written their flat numbers on the bins, even though each bin was supposed to be for one specific flat. I knew which one was mine because it was the one that was brand new, because I had to buy one when I moved in. That's right. If you think seven bins for eight flats was bad, there used to only be six.

I thought it would be obvious to everybody which bin was mine, but people would dump their bags in it anyway. So I got a pen and wrote my flat number on the lid, and then it stopped. Well, almost stopped. The students that lived downstairs, in the flat that Nick's now in, they'd still sometimes dump their bags in my bin, even though my flat number was on it. They didn't do it as often as before, but they still did it.

But then they moved out, and I thought it would stop there. But then Nick moves in. And a week after he moved in, I came down here with a bag. I opened my bin, the one with Flat 3/1 written on it, and instead of seeing an empty bin, it was full. I tore open the bag to see if I could find an envelope, to see an address. Not that I would ever do anything, not that I would take the envelope to the person's door to show that I'd caught them, because I don't think you're allowed to open somebody's bin bags, even if they're in your own bin. But I wanted to know.

I ripped open the black bin liner at the top of my bin, and accidentally wiped my finger in something wet. I pulled my finger out and looked at it, thinking that the stuff on my finger was maybe porridge or mushroom soup. But when I smelled it, I boked. I looked in the bag, and saw that I'd put my finger in a used nappy.

Think of how that would make you feel.

I shut the bin lid and looked at my flat number on it, in case it wasn't clear, but it was as clear as crystal. The lid was a bit dirty, and the black pen didn't stand out that much against the green, but it was clear enough. Flat 3/1. Nobody else had their number on their bin, and yet here were somebody else's bags in my bin. And they were Nick's bags, because nobody else had a wean, nobody else wore nappies.

But I gave him the benefit of the doubt. I can't quite work out how you could make a mistake like that, putting your bags in a bin that have an address on it that is so clearly not yours, but I gave him the benefit of the doubt anyway. Or more accurately, I just told myself to try and not care. I had to do that. I could feel acid in my stomach. I could feel my heart getting sore. I took the bin bag back up to my flat and I dumped it in the cupboard until my bin was empty again. But it started to make my flat stink.

I tried to chill out, I didn't want it all flaring up again, I had to tell myself to just share and share alike. But it's hard to be like that when your flat is stinking because somebody else is using your bin. But I told myself to share and share alike. At the time I thought that Nick could turn out to be a friend, or, at the very least, a friendly neighbour. But he made it clear that he wasn't interested in being either, he made it so fucking hard.

I bumped into him about a week later, on the stairs, and this time he was carrying his son. I said hello to Nick, then I said hello to his son. I said it in that baby talk way. I said, 'Oh, hello, and what's your name?' That was hard for me to do, because I don't really know how to talk to weans, I don't have one myself, I've never known one. But I made an effort. I wanted to keep things light and friendly, because I had something to say about the bin, and I thought that saying hello to the boy would be a good way to start. So I said hello, but the wean said nothing back, which was all right, weans tend to do that. They sometimes just look back and wait for their mum or dad to tell them it's all right to speak to the stranger. But did Nick do that? Did Nick tell his son to go ahead and talk to the nice man from upstairs? No. And you'd think that Nick would at least then tell me his son's name, having heard me ask. You'd think he'd be friendly towards the man whose bin he dumped his son's used nappies into. Or not even friendly, just polite. You'd think that, would you? But he wasn't. He isn't interested in friendship or politeness. He just kept on walking down the stairs with his son.

I didn't get upset, though, I didn't let it show. I kept it light, because I still wanted to say my thing about the bin. I said, 'Excuse me.' When I said it, Nick's son looked at me, but Nick didn't, even though he heard me. So I said 'Nick'. I didn't like doing that, saying his name, because it was like I was trying to get friendly with him, and I knew he wasn't interested. He's the type of person that seems to be disgusted by friendship. I remember feeling my pulse racing when I said it, and my hands were probably shaking. I remember yawning to try and make it look like none of it was a big deal, that's the type of person I am, that's how much this bin situation was getting to me.

Nick looked around, but kept on walking. So I said, 'I noticed that you don't have a bin. Do you want me to phone the council for you and order one?'

Nick said, 'Naw, mate, you're all right,' and away he went.

That was that, then. That was that. I tried, and it was utterly horrible.

I went up to my flat, and I'll tell you, I was shaking. I didn't know what to do. I know that might seem like an overreaction over something that seems so trivial, but there was just nothing I could do about the situation I was in, he just wasn't interested in reaching a solution.

I waited a few days and tried to just not think about it. Then I went out and bought a tin of paint, a tin of white paint, thinking that maybe the writing on the bin wasn't clear enough. I wrote Flat 3/1 on the top, bigger than what I'd written before in ink. I wrote 'flat' in lower case, rather than caps, so that it didn't look too shouty. And I wrote it on the front of the bin as well. And on the left, and the right. There was nothing else I could do. What else could I do that would say 'Please, please don't use my bin'?

I came home one afternoon. I opened the front door to the block and I was about to head upstairs to my flat, when I saw that the door to the back garden was open. The door is always shut, unless somebody opens it to go out into the garden, and the reason for that was usually to go out to the bins.

I walked up the stairs and saw that the door to Nick's flat was open. So I went up the stairs two at a time to the landing between the second and third floor, to stand at the window that looked out to the back garden. And there was Nick, walking towards the bins with a bin bag.

There are seven bins. Seven. And one of them has Flat 3/1 written on it. Nick knows that he is in Flat 2/1, don't think for a second that he doesn't know that. I wondered once if he had got himself mixed up with what number the ground floor is. The ground floor is 0. But if he thinks that the ground floor is 1, then he'd think that two floors up – where he lives – is called floor 3. He would think he was in Flat 3/1 instead of

2/1. But there is no way that he thinks that. He must have Flat 2/1 written on every letter addressed to him, he must be able to see from everybody else's nameplate on their door. None of that matters anyway, he knows that he didn't write his address in white paint on his bin. He knows that the bin with Flat 3/1 written on it is my bin.

And yet guess what bin he put his bag in? Guess what bin he made a beeline for, without even thinking twice about it? You guessed it.

When I saw him do that, I said 'You fucking prick'. It felt so good just to get that out. He didn't hear me, it was nothing more than a whisper and the window was closed. But it felt so good. I said, 'You fucking, fucking prick. Nick the prick.'

And then I heard a voice from behind me say 'Futtin pritt'.

The fright it gave me. I turned around and it was Nick's wee boy. He was watching me, from just outside his door. He was standing there in a onesie, and he said 'Futting pritt' and 'Nit the pritt'. He didn't know what he was saying.

For a second, I thought about saying something to the boy, something to try and convince him to say something else. But I knew it was over. I knew that was it. There was no point. I turned to look out the window towards the bin area, and before I even laid eyes on

Nick I just knew that he'd be looking at me, I just knew he would. I looked down and he was looking back. I just knew that would happen.

I walked away from the window and I walked up the stairs to my door. I didn't run. There was no point.

I got into my flat and closed the front door. I opened it again to close the storm doors outside then close the front door again, so that I was behind two sets of doors. There was no point in doing that either, so I don't know why I did.

I sat on a cushion that I've got next to the kitchen window and I looked out the bin area at the back, waiting for my door to be knocked. And then it did. It went knock knock knock. Then it got a bang. Then a bang bang bang. Then he went away.

But he'll be back. At some point, he'll be back.

So I waited until it was dark, then I came out here, to the back garden. I opened my bin, I took out Nick's bags, then I climbed in and shut the lid.

That's why I'm here. There's nowhere else to go. You can see that there's just nowhere else for me to go.

And when he finds me, either tomorrow morning or whenever he finds me, he'll get the message. They'll all get the message.

This is my bin.

Mine.

The Other Side
of the Counter

Hugh was sick of that lot.

There had been another attack. Another bombing, down in London. And he was fucking sick of them. Not just the ones that did the bombing, but all of them. The lot of them. Even the ones at the shops. Even the ones in Ali's up the road.

'After everything we've done for them,' he'd tell his mates.

He'd tell his family as well. He'd tell his sons and anybody they brought around. He'd go to things, go to parties, and he'd tell anybody there. Anybody that agreed with him, he'd keep chatting to. Anybody that didn't, well, they could fuck off, if they didn't want to believe the facts.

They hate us.

'They hate us, you know.'

He could tell when he went to their shops. Even in Ali's. He could feel them bottling it up. He'd get a smile most of the time, he'd get a smile and a chat and a hello and a goodbye, oh, they'd give him all that. Ali was the nicest guy in the world.

But then Hugh would read the paper, and there it was. A picture of carnage, telling you what they really think of us.

He asked his mates: 'What I don't get is why? Why? What have we done?'

The night after the attack, his wife Carol took him to a charity quiz. They were put in a team with some folk that he didn't know, and he got chatting. He pointed to Carol and said to the guy next to him, 'She goes to the shop, and they're the nicest people you could imagine. You'd think they were your best pals, your best friends in the whole wide world. Isn't that right, Carol?'

Carol said, 'They are nice, Hugh. Ali's nice. Ali's got nothing to do with that stuff down south. Most of them have got nothing to do with that stuff down south. D'you really think Ali wants to kill us? It's ridiculous.'

It got him fuming when she tried all that. He never raised his voice, but he was fuming. He wasn't fuming at her, he was fuming at how they'd tricked his wife, even though it was all there in black and white, if she only bothered to open her fucking eyes.

Then, one day, he said, 'You know what I'm gonnae do?' He was sitting in the pub with his mates, while Carol was back in the house. He put his drink down on the table and said to everybody around him, 'You know what I'm gonnae do? And I mean this.'

'What?' said his mate Graeme. Graeme couldn't fucking stand that lot either.

'I'm gonnae open up a shop,' said Hugh. 'You know that wee cafe that shut down, the one right next to Ali's?'

'Aye,' said his other mate Ross. 'Are you serious?'

'Aye I'm fucking serious,' said Hugh. 'I'm gonnae buy it, or rent it, or, I don't know how you go about it, but I'm gonnae do it. I'm gonnae drive the cunt out of business.'

His pals laughed, but he told them he meant what he said. He was serious. And they realised how serious he was when they saw him inspecting the building.

'What the fuck's this?' asked Graeme, when he saw Hugh inside the empty cafe with another guy. Graeme was passing by on his way to Ali's.

'I told you,' said Hugh. 'I'm serious. Will you help me? Will you help me get the word out? Tell everybody that there's a new shop opening up. A good white shop. But don't say white. You know what I mean.'

'I know,' said Graeme. 'You're a good man.'

'D'you know what I mean, Graeme? I'm not saying they're all terrorists. I'm not saying that the terrorists are terrorists because they urnae white, I'm not saying that. I'm just giving people a choice.'

'I know,' said Graeme. 'You're a good man, Hugh, I've been wanting this for years.'

A month or so later, Hugh was all set, ready to pull the shutters up for the very first time. He had his very own newsagent's. It was unbelievable, when he thought about it.

He'd needed a lot of help. A lot of advice. Once he sent the word out about what he was doing and why, he couldn't believe the support he got. Nobody could come right out and say it, though, you couldn't just come out and say it these days. But there were a lot of good people who'd had it up to here. He'd remind them of the bombings. They'd tell him they knew, they were on his side. Good on him.

He even got help from Ali himself. How was that for two-faced?

While Hugh was renovating the place, Ali would say good morning, and Hugh would smile and say good morning back. Oh, it was all smiles and hellos and 'All the best with your new shop, let me know if need any stock', and you'd fall for it. You'd be taken in. You'd be taken in by the good manners, by the please and thank yous. But here's what was also considered good manners: saying sorry. It was good manners to say sorry for something you'd done, and Hugh could never recall Ali apologising for any of the stuff down south. Not once.

But there would be no need to apologise if they didn't do it in the first place. Hugh still didn't understand why. Why did they do it? Why? After everything we've done for them. After everything he'd done for Ali. Buying his stuff, buying his food and milk, giving him business on a daily business, giving business to the lot of them. Then the lot of them want to blow you up? These customers, these people that you get to know so well, you can look them in the eyes and want to blow them up? How? Why? Well, it didn't matter. He wouldn't be giving him business anymore. In fact, he'd be taking it, and it would be a pleasure.

Hugh finally opened his shop.

He opened it on a Sunday. A Sunday morning, up at the crack of dawn, making sure everything was perfect, making sure there was enough rolls and milk and bread and everything else that people wanted for their breakfast.

He was worried that nobody would come, that they'd stick with what they knew and go next door instead. But he was wrong to worry. There was a queue at the door when he opened up. A queue. When had you ever heard of a queue at a newsagent's?

He opened the door. Graeme and Ross were at the front and gave a cheer, and the folk behind cheered along.

In came the customers, into his shop. But it was more than a shop. People didn't just buy their things and go. They'd stay for a chat. He knew he'd made something special. A community. Graeme and Ross and half a dozen more of them stood around near the till, chatting. Speaking their mind. They had to keep it down, though. They had to kick the front door shut in case the talk floated out to the street, because not everybody in the world would agree with what they had to say. You know how it is these days.

The excitement of the first day came to an end. As the days rolled on, things began to settle. There was never a queue again, but there were still a fair number of people through the door in the morning, in to get their stuff for breakfast.

And you had to see the state of them. The state of them that early in the morning. He'd never seen them like that before, and he had to hold back a laugh for the first couple of weeks.

Some of them would come in wearing their pyjamas and slippers. That's not something that Hugh had ever done himself, he'd never walked out the door wearing the stuff that was just for wearing about the house. But in they'd come, wearing their pyjamas, or stuff they wore as pyjamas, like a done-in pair of joggy bottoms, all baggy at the knees with a bit of chocolate on the leg.

He was getting to know them better, in a funny sort of way. He'd see women coming in, women he'd see at the pub who were normally dolled up with make-up, now with nothing on their face except for a drool at the side of their mouth and all that crusty yellow sleep in their eyes. It was like he was waking up with them all, the women and the men, like he lived with them, getting to see the real person before they got themselves polished.

He'd get people in who'd normally never have a hair out of place. People who'd normally have their hair done up with stuff in it, or combed or straightened or curled, but in they'd come with it sticking up at one side and flat at the other. Some of them would give their hair a wee fix at the front as they came in the door, but they forgot about the back. They'd walk past the counter and turn away down the aisle on their way towards the fridge, and Hugh would get a good look at their hair at the back. It would be flat against the back of their head, because their head had been lying on a pillow all night, and there would be this wiggly side parting that ran up the back of the head from the neck to the crown. Hugh began to notice that some of them looked like the back end of a dog. His pal Graeme was one of them. The wiggly side parting at the back looked like the space between a dog's hind legs. The crown, where all the hair parted away to show the scalp, looked like the dog's arsehole. It looked like these dogs with the curly-up tails that put their arseholes right on show. Once you got that picture in your head, it was hard to unsee it.

What a state they were. If only they knew. Maybe they did, and it was a sign that they were comfortable around him, that they didn't feel the need to get done up to the nines just to nip round to his shop. They'd come over with the sleep in their eyes and with their hair a mess, wearing their joggy bottoms that were all baggy at the knees or with a bit of chocolate on them that didn't get washed off for weeks. They felt comfortable enough to just fall out of bed and walk around to Hugh's before bothering to make themselves decent or do their hair or brush their teeth.

And that was something that they all had in common. None of them seemed to brush their teeth. Not before coming to the shop anyway.

He used to do the same thing himself. It made sense. People went to the shops to get stuff for breakfast, and if you brushed your teeth before having breakfast then you'd go to work with your breakfast on your breath. It made sense to just brush them afterwards.

He knew they didn't brush their teeth, because he could smell it.

Even with him being behind the counter and them on the other side, he could still smell it. The breath would drift over and reach his nose. That morning breath. They all had it. Most of them smelled roughly the same, but some of them were different from the rest. Some of them would have a sour milk smell to it. Some were more tobacco-y. There was a boy in his twenties who would come in, and Hugh thought the boy must have that halitosis. Hugh could have shut his eyes and told you when the boy walked in the door, just by the smell of his breath. He could have done it with a few of them. His pal Ross's bird had an eggy morning breath, but it didn't smell like she'd been eating eggs somehow, it smelled like that's just the way it was. He got to smell hers up close once, when she couldn't find the tins of soup. He had to come out from behind the counter to show her. He pointed at them, to show her that they were right in front of her, and she laughed in his face with that breath and said that she must be needing glasses.

He got to know them all really well, really quickly, and a lot better than he would have if he hadn't opened his shop.

Five months later, there was another attack, down south. Another bombing. It was in the papers. The pictures. The bodies. It was the worst yet, said the front pages, in terms of numbers.

Hugh opened his shop that morning, and waited inside until he heard Ali arrive to open up next door. Hugh gave it a minute, then he walked out, checking across the street and behind him to make sure the coast was clear, before walking into Ali's.

He saw Ali looking at the front pages. Even though the door had beeped, Ali didn't look up right away. When he did, he pointed to the papers and shook his head. He was about to say something.

Hugh stopped him and said, 'You don't need to, mate. I get it. I get it, and it's cool.'

Cupid

There was this lassie that John was seeing. He wasn't going out with her, he was just seeing her. Seeing her around, from a distance. But he wanted to go out with her. He didn't know her, he never spoke to her. And he wanted to change that.

He first saw her cycling down Great Western Road, free-wheeling down towards the Botanic Gardens. He stopped in his tracks to watch her go by. He stopped so quickly that a guy walked into the back of him and tutted. John remembered that she had green tights on, that first time he saw her. That wasn't all he liked about her, but he liked that for some reason. Green tights.

Then he saw her on Great Western Road again a few days later. He didn't notice or care what she was wearing that second time. All he thought was, 'There's that lassie again. Who is she?'

The next place he saw her was down at Dumbarton Road, which wasn't far from Great Western Road, so he thought she must stay up the west end. But then he saw her up the toon, at the Merchant City. He saw her for just a second as she turned down one of the streets there.

Wherever he saw her, she was always on her bike. He wanted to stop her and ask her name, but he couldn't, because of her bike. And he didn't have one himself.

He partly wished that she didn't have a bike, but her bike was part of what made her beautiful. It was to do with how she looked when she was on it, when she was cycling. She didn't wear a helmet, which was a dangerous thing to do, and he liked that. It showed she was carefree. Everybody wore helmets these days, and she didn't. Which showed she was different. And not having a helmet also let the wind in her hair. She had long hair. Her hair was full, as they said in the adverts. Full and thick, and a bit wavy. Like Shakira's.

But what was her name? Who was she? John wanted to know.

He shouted on her once when she was going by, but he saw that she was wearing earphones, which was another dangerous thing he liked. He wondered what she was listening to.

He just wanted to maybe ask her out. He at least wanted to be in the same place as her and just say a few words, to just say hello. He wanted to find out where she lived.

If he knew where she lived, then he could stand himself around the corner, and walk her way, then bump into her and get talking.

Or he could wait in some of the places that she probably went to that were near her house, like a shop or a cafe or the nearest park. There wasn't any guarantee that she'd go to a cafe near her house, seeing as she had a bike. She could go anywhere on that, and he himself didn't like going to the local cafes that were near where he lived, he preferred the ones up the west end. But she would surely jump over to her local corner shop now and then. And she wouldn't take her bike for that. She'd just walk over, and he'd be able to talk to her then.

But he didn't know where she lived, and he couldn't find out, because he just couldn't get talking to her while she was on that bike. He also couldn't just chase after her, or jump in a taxi and say 'Follow that lassie!' like they did in films. That would put her off.

Or maybe it wouldn't.

Maybe she'd appreciate the effort. He didn't know. He'd seen programmes where lassies liked being 'courted', if that was the word. But he didn't want to do all that chasing about. He wanted her to just stop for a while, for a chat.

Then his opportunity came.

He was walking down a street near Byres Road, kind of halfway between Dumbarton Road and Great Western Road. It was a wide street, but pretty quiet at that time of day. And he was thinking about her. He was actually thinking about her just before this happened. Then he saw somebody cycling his way, and he wondered if it was her.

And it actually was her.

It was the perfect chance, but there was little he could do. She was at the other side of the street, not on his side where he would have been in her line of sight and he could smile at her and make her stop.

There was no point in shouting over to her, because she had her earphones in again. And he didn't want to wave his arms about, because she'd maybe think he was trying to alert her to there being something wrong with her bike, like a wobbly wheel, and when she stopped and saw that nothing was wrong, she might feel like he'd wasted her time or got speaking to her under false pretences. He didn't want that. He didn't want that to be her first impression of him.

He didn't know what to do. He walked backwards, looking at her, and stumbled into a bag full of rubbish. He nearly fell.

He regained his balance and looked across the road at her quickly to see if he'd made himself look clumsy.

It would maybe be a good thing to look like that – he'd seen in some films that some women liked guys who were clumsy, the type of guys that trip over their feet or fall over things. But she didn't see him.

He looked at the bag of rubbish again. It was part of a larger pile of rubbish, a pile of things that people had dumped outside their flats for the binmen to pick up. Unwanted odds and ends. There was an old-style telly, there were some ornaments and lamps, and there was one of those Vileda Supermops, with the mop head all dirty and used.

As he looked at it all, he got the idea that it might be good to chuck something at her.

He didn't want to hurt her, or even hit her, he just wanted whatever he chucked to land in front of her, to get her attention.

He was thinking of chucking one of the ornaments, and he'd time it just right so that she didn't see him throw it. Then she'd turn around to see who threw it, and he'd look behind him like somebody else threw it, and then she'd come over and they'd both get chatting about it, and he'd maybe ask her what her name was and where she lived.

But he picked up the mop instead.

He threw it towards her like a javelin. He didn't want to hit her, so he aimed a short distance ahead. There was no point in aiming behind her, she wouldn't see it if it landed behind. He aimed ahead, and hoped that he didn't hit her.

But what if he did?

What if he hit her, what would she think of that? Would she get the police? Or would she think it was romantic in a way? Wouldn't it be romantic to go to that effort, to actually pick something up and throw it at her, in a caveman sort of way? The mop was like a spear. Or an arrow.

Like Cupid's arrow.

Wouldn't that be a story to tell?

Imagine she was telling their children the story of how they met, and she told them that. Or on a game show, where the host sometimes asks couples how they met. She'd tell the audience that she was hit by Cupid's arrow, in a manner of speaking. Then she'd say it was actually a mop.

The mop flew through the air, and landed between the spokes of her front wheel. The pole of the mop jammed against the fork, causing the front wheel to come to an immediate halt. She flew over the handlebars, and for a moment she looked like Supergirl.

It reminded him of a time when he was a boy. He had asked the people in the video shop if he could have the Supergirl poster on the wall, but they didn't give him it.

The lassie bashed her head against the back of a parked car, and didn't get up.

John ran over to her, looking around as he ran, to see who saw what happened, but nobody was around.

He tried speaking to her. He asked her what her name was, but she was out for the count. The contents of her bag were spilled everywhere, and he saw her purse. He opened it up and pulled out one of her bank cards, and saw her name. He'd preferred to have seen an envelope lying about with her name and address, so he could find out where she lived, but her name was enough for now.

He phoned an ambulance and took the mop back to where it was, and then he ran away.

The next day, he phoned around the hospitals to see where she was. He told them her name, now that he knew it, and told them that she was his girlfriend.

It was a lie, but it felt nice. He was glad he did it. He almost wasn't going to. Before making the phone calls, he was worried that if he said that she was his girlfriend, it would show in his voice that he was lying and they'd trace the call. But they believed him. And there was something in that.

He paid her a visit. She was still unconscious, thankfully. He was thankful, because he wasn't yet up for telling her about the mop.

About Cupid's arrow.

What a story that would be to tell everybody.

First he'd have to tell her, though.

But not yet. Something in his gut was telling him: not yet.

The Dog

Ben sat in his boardroom with Julie and the clients, looking at her presentation on the 50-inch screen on the wall.

Looking at it.

He couldn't say that he was watching it.

He was looking at it, looking in that direction. If any of the people there in the room were to have glanced at him, and he was sure that they had, it would have looked like he was watching it, and taking an interest. At least, he hoped it looked that way. He reminded himself that there was no reason for them to think otherwise, there was no reason for anybody to think that he wasn't focused and in the room 110 per cent. The clients would assume he was, because it was his company, after all. And Julie would assume that he was enthusiastic about this potentially huge cash cow. There had been a few ups and downs, but things were picking up, and they'd pick up even more with this job in the door.

'It's a big one,' Julie had said last Wednesday, after the client made their first phone call. 'They're looking for a new website, new identity, branding …' She began counting out the individual pieces of work on her fingers. 'They're asking if we can do the copywriting for their social *media*, they'll be looking at *print*, you know, *posters*, *advertising*, and so on.'

And so on. Another big job in the door.

When Julie had told him about the call, he'd said 'Yessss!' and thudded his fist in mid-air. But did he care? Did he really care that much? Of course he didn't. But did anybody? He wasn't sure if anybody really cared that much. It was just for show, wasn't it? Julie seemed to care, though, but she hadn't been doing this for as long as him.

That was maybe all it was. Maybe he'd just been doing this for a long time. Ask anybody who'd been doing the same job for 20 years if they still had the same get up and go as when they first started. It couldn't be many.

Ben nodded at Julie as she continued with her presentation. Julie pointed to some stats on the screen and said something about unique visitors. She looked to Ben and said a number. Ben nodded, then looked at the clients and nodded at them as well. He made sure he had nodded throughout the presentation, but not continuously. He would nod for a while, then slowly stop nodding, then later begin nodding again. He paced it so that the nodding drifted in and out like the tide.

'And so,' said Julie, 'that concludes our presentation. We'll be happy to answer any questions.'

Julie looked to Ben, to gauge how well the pitch went. He smiled and nodded, opening his eyes wide for a brief moment, to send a message along the lines of 'Wow!' It didn't match how he felt, but that wasn't a reflection on Julie, he was sure she did very well. But whatever the reason for how he was feeling, Julie didn't deserve to bear the brunt of that, so he gave her the smile and flashed her the eyes. She smiled back.

The clients began asking their questions, and Ben was thankful that most of them were questions that Julie was better equipped to answer. Project-manager questions. Questions regarding timescales, how soon this or that could be started, if there were enough staff to carry out the jobs simultaneously or if they have to be done one after the other. But he backed her up with a nod here and there.

Was he maybe coming across as too quiet?

He picked a moment to say something. He didn't want Julie thinking that he was a bit quiet. He didn't want her telling other people later. That could lead to people asking if he was all right, and he didn't want any of that.

He was all right. He was. Anyway, even if he wasn't, how do you put something like that into words?

Things were going very, very well. And they'll be going even better when they got this job in the door.

'We really have a great team here,' he said, as he looked through the glass wall that separated the board-room from the rest of the office. The office was looking great. They'd just had another paint job, it was much better than the one before. More modern. Fresher, cleaner, more crisp. Ben nodded slowly as he surveyed the 30 or so staff who were busy on their computers, then looked back to Julie and said, 'Great bunch of guys.'

They left the boardroom and walked over to Sarah at reception, to order a taxi for the clients. This is where the small talk usually happened, during the minute or two before the taxi arrived. He wasn't sure if he could do it. Sometimes it took ten minutes. Sometimes it took longer because there was a mistake resulting in the taxi company not sending a taxi and they had to be phoned again.

He really wasn't sure if he could do it. Not today. If he could have come up with a good enough excuse to get away, he would have, something about being too busy to talk. A thousand apologies, but he was simply too busy. Then he would rush off to his room or out the door. But nothing came to mind. Nothing that Julie wouldn't see through. Nothing that wouldn't make her wonder.

'So,' he said.

Julie and the clients looked at him.

He looked away, towards the office, and then out the window to the city below.

'So,' he said again.

His eyes followed a bird in the distance, as it flew far, far away.

'Are you guys heading back to the airport?' he asked.

He turned back towards them all, his eyebrows raised, his lips pursed. He reckoned it was just the right expression for a question like that. A small-talk question. He didn't want to look overly interested to know the answer. If he looked too interested to hear the answer to a question so unimportant, it wouldn't look right. It would look too smiley. He'd always thought that people like that were hiding something.

'The airport?' said one of the clients, the woman. 'Not right away.' She looked at her phone quickly to check the time. Ben couldn't remember her name, or the name of her male colleague. One of them had a Gaelic-sounding name, but he couldn't remember if it was her or him. He hoped he wasn't put in a position where he was shown up for not knowing.

'We've got another couple of hours,' said the man. 'We had another meeting booked in, but it fell through.' He smiled and looked out the window. He seemed happy to have the spare time. Ben looked at him, and had a vague memory of that feeling. A vague memory of having that spare time, and knowing what to do with it.

The female client wasn't so happy, and asked Ben and Julie if they had heard of the agency they were due to meet. Oh, Julie knew them very well, and assured the clients that they had dodged a bullet. Julie shared her stories, speaking quietly to avoid letting the rest of the staff hear her throw mud at one of their rivals.

Ben kept quiet. It wasn't that he found bad-mouthing to be unprofessional. Five or ten years ago, he would have capitalised on the spare couple of hours to take the clients back into the boardroom, fetch them a coffee, and proceed to trash every other agency in the UK.

But now, he preferred to look out the window, nodding, and repeating the occasional word that Julie said.

'… and the way they then tried to brush it under the carpet was awful,' said Julie, looking at Ben.

'Awful,' said Ben, shaking his head. 'Just awful.'

'Sorry to interrupt,' said Sarah at the reception desk, putting down her phone. She looked at the clients. 'That's your taxi here.'

'Good,' said Ben, hoping that it didn't sound like he was saying it was good that the chitchat had come to an end, even though it was. He thought about making a joke about how it sounded like he was glad to see them go, but decided not to.

Ben and Julie walked them to the door.

'Just that button there,' said Ben, pointing to the button on the wall that let them out.

'Thank you,' said the female client, pressing the button and pushing the door open.

'We'll get you down,' said Ben, hoping they would say no.

'No, it's all right.'

'Okay, if you're sure,' said Ben. 'Look forward to hearing from you. Safe journey.'

Julie showed them out the door to the lift while Ben stayed in the office, next to the reception desk. He was happy with that final goodbye. If there was any doubt in Julie's mind that he was a bit quiet, that would help her forget all that. That was a friendly goodbye. It was talkative.

Julie returned through the door. She looked over her shoulder to make sure the door had shut. When she saw that it had, she gave Ben a grin and two thumbs up.

'I think it went really well,' she said. 'What do you think?'

'I think it went really well,' he said. Then, realising he had just repeated what she had said, he added a bit more. 'I think they'll go for it.'

'Oh, I hope so.' Julie turned towards Sarah, who had her phone in her hand. 'Sarah, sorry. Could you send a meeting invite out?'

Another meeting.

'Sure,' said Sarah, putting down the phone and turning towards her computer. She put her hands on the keyboard and looked to Julie for the details.

'Ummm, in half an hour?' said Julie, looking at Ben. 'I think we'll get everyone in? Luke and Ahmed, Lynn, Isla. Shane as well. Uhhh, who else?' She thought for a moment, then waved her hands. 'Oh, that'll be enough. If we need anybody else, we'll let them know.'

Ben heard her say 'Are you all right, Ben?'

He looked up from the floor quickly. Why did she ask that?

He felt his face tingle. 'What?'

'I said is that all right?'

'Oh, yeah, that's fine. Sorry, I was too busy thinking about …'

Think of something.

'… if the meeting also needs …'

Needs what?

'… Nathan.'

Nathan was in the back-end team, doing the server side scripting. There would be a lot of that needed if they were to land the job, so it was a good call. Providing that Nathan still worked there. Ben really hoped that Nathan still worked there.

'Nathan?' said Julie. 'Oh yeah, Nathan as well.' She looked at Sarah, who gave her keyboard a rattle to add Nathan's email address to the invite. 'And that's it.'

'Okay,' said Sarah. 'That's it sent. Meeting at 11 a.m.'

Ben turned to Julie. 'See you then,' he said. Then he turned and walked away.

It was important that he walked away first. If he didn't, Julie would have walked away, and he would have been left standing twiddling his thumbs in front of Sarah. And Sarah would have seen it. It might have looked like he simply had nothing to do at that moment, but there was a chance she'd sense that the aimlessness was something else.

Just keep moving.

He began walking down the length of the office, down the aisle that ran through the middle of the room. He walked slowly. There was no reason to walk fast, there was nowhere to go. It was a dead end.

He looked to the left, and saw Jack, working on a design for a website. Ben assumed it was a website. He walked over. Jack was new here. He was young and still quite timid. He wouldn't give Ben any trouble.

'That's looking great,' said Ben.

'Thanks, sir.'

Holly leaned to the side of her monitor to give Jack a smile.

'Sir?' she said, laughing. 'Did you say "sir"?'

Jack's face went red. He was barely out of school. 'Sorry,' he said. 'Ben.'

Jack looked embarrassed, but not embarrassed enough to stop him from smiling and giving Holly the finger. Ben wanted to put his hand on Jack's shoulder and laugh along, but then he'd have to say something funny. He'd have to say some kind of punchline, something to put the icing on the cake.

He put his hand on Jack's shoulder, and took a breath in preparation for what he was going to say.

But he had nothing to say.

He could feel Jack's shoulder move away slightly from under his hand.

Do something.

'Oh,' said Ben, and he turned away, as if he had just remembered somebody that he had to speak to. A thousand apologies. He suddenly remembered that he needed to speak to somebody. Somebody at the other side of the office. And who would that be? He decided it would be Faye.

He wandered away, clicking his fingers, to give the impression of a man remembering something, and began walking towards Faye. And who knows, maybe when he got there, he really would have something to say to her.

She was sitting at one of the desks across the aisle. He walked over to her. Then he got to her. Then he kept on walking.

He walked to the window.

He looked out the window to the streets below, and wondered if he was being watched by Jack or Holly behind him. They didn't know that his intention was to speak to Faye, so he was probably fine. If he'd said, 'Oh, I need to speak to Faye,' but they saw him walk past Faye, then they'd maybe wonder what was up with that.

He tried to see them in the reflection of the window, but he couldn't. It was too bright outside.

What did he look like right now?

What was he doing?

He needed to turn around.

He turned around to face the employees again. They were busy, working away, walking here and there. Luke was opening a box. Louise was throwing something in the bin. Bobby was showing Raymond something that looked like a toy, a figure from a game or a cartoon.

If they looked at him now, they would see he was standing there doing nothing. Nothing at all. Nothing to do, nowhere to go. Lost.

Ben let out an unintentional high-pitched whine: 'Hmmmm.'

It sounded like somebody letting air out of a balloon. He wasn't even sure if it had come from him, until Faye's head turned away from her screen to look at him.

He changed the whine into a tune. He was just humming a tune, that's all. He didn't look at her. He hummed his tune and clicked his fingers and walked away to the toilet and closed the door behind him and locked it.

For a while, he stood there, facing the door. He looked at the white paint. He looked at the brush strokes. There was a small drip around eye level, where the paint had been put on too thick, and now it was stuck that way. He pushed his thumbnail against it, to see if it was soft, but it wasn't.

He put his hands by his side and leaned his forehead against the drip, enjoying the cooling feeling of the door, and he let out a sigh. The cool feeling on his head began to warm up, then that part of his head became hot. He rolled his head slightly so that his left temple rested against another part of the door, and it was cool again. After a while, that part of his head also became hot. He began rolling his head slowly to the other side, to cool his right temple.

He was interrupted by somebody trying to open the door. He didn't move until he heard them go away. He needed to leave, but not too soon. If he left too soon, people would know he wasn't in to do the toilet. He waited until he'd stayed there long enough for the average person to do the toilet then wash their hands. He took a deep breath and stood tall, then he unlocked the door and walked out.

And there again was the office.

He could walk back into the toilet and walk back out again a million times, and here it would be.

This was it.

He walked over to Sarah at the reception desk.

'Sarah,' he said.

Sarah finished typing a few more words, then looked at him and smiled. 'Yeah?'

He smiled back. 'I'm going to be out for a while. Maybe an hour or so. I'll be back in around an hour.'

'Okay,' said Sarah. And then: 'No. Wait. Remember you have the meeting at 11. In about 20 minutes.'

No.

That's what she said. She said no.

He remembered when he started the company. Why he started the company. It wasn't to be told no. It was to enable him to come and go as he pleased. It wasn't to be told no, you can't go. But it didn't quite turn out like that, did it?

No.

'I see,' said Ben. 'Thanks for reminding me. I'm just going to step out for something, but I'll be back in time for the meeting. What time is the meeting again, 11? 11's fine, I'll be back in time for 11.'

'Okay,' said Sarah. 'But I'll let everyone know that you might be a bit late, if you're held up.'

'No, no,' said Ben. 'I won't be late. 11 is fine. Bye.'

He walked to the door, pressed the button that let him out, and out he walked to the corridor.

He had nowhere to go.

Ben pressed the button for the lift. He was six floors up, and he could see from the display that the lift was on the fourth floor.

And now it was on the third. It was going down.

The waiting around gave his mind time to think.

Where are you going? Go back to the office, you have a meeting in 20 minutes. In fact, it's probably 19 minutes now.

He took the stairs.

He reached the ground floor and walked out into the foyer.

'Hi Ben,' said somebody. 'Early lunch?'

It was the guy from the company downstairs on the

fifth floor. The guy from the travel company. Gordon. He was standing by the lift.

'Yeah,' said Ben, with no intention of going on an early lunch. He smiled at Gordon and nodded and put his finger on his lips to say 'Shhhhh', like it was their naughty wee secret. Ben thought that Gordon would appreciate that, he seemed like a fun type of guy. That's the impression that Ben got from him. Or maybe it was just to do with his line of business. Travel. Holidays. He seemed like a fun type of guy when he came up to Ben's office a while back, when he came up with that offer. The offer was that if Ben's team built the website for his travel company, Ben and the team would receive a really good discount on some fantastic holidays. Ben had said it sounded great, but they were extremely busy. In truth, they weren't that busy. Ben just wasn't interested. Interested in holidays. Gordon made it sound like fun, but Ben knew from experience that it wasn't. Not for him. He'd been on holiday and his head went with him.

But an early lunch? Ben liked the sound of that. No, he wasn't planning on going on one, but he liked that it was Gordon's first thought. He liked that way of thinking.

Maybe Ben could speak to him. Maybe Gordon was the person to speak to. Maybe Gordon knew more about all this than anybody. It was his business. People getting away. People needing to just go away. People going away, not to do work in a more relaxed surrounding, but going away for the sake of going away.

'D'you care to join me?' asked Ben.

'I wish,' said Gordon, as the lift door opened. 'Another time. You free next week?'

'I don't know.'

Ben wasn't interested in next week. He thought Gordon was the type of person who would walk away from the lift and drop everything, but he wasn't.

'Okay,' said Gordon. 'Well, I'll skip up next week and you can tell us how the old schedule's looking.' He smiled and walked into the lift, and the door closed. Ben stood there in the empty foyer, thinking about how pale the guy looked for a person who sold holidays.

He walked out the door, down the ramp to the car park, and got in his car.

He didn't look at the clock on the dashboard. He made sure he didn't. He had minutes, he knew that. He had minutes to do whatever it was he was going to do, before it was time to be back at the meeting.

Go back to the meeting.

Get out the car and go back to the office. This is a big job and it'll be very good. Very good for you and very good for the company. You'll be in solid work for the next two years.

THE DOG

He turned the key, started the engine, and drove away.

He took a left out the car park and down the hill towards the main road. He waited at the lines for a couple of buses to go past.

Where are you going? Wherever you go, you'll have to make that same journey back. However long it'll take you to get there, double it. That's how long you'll need. Forget it.

He indicated to go right, which he usually did when sitting at the bottom of the hill. That was the way home.

He turned left.

A car behind him beeped its horn. Ben gave the person a wave.

He continued to drive. These roads weren't as well known to him as the roads to the right, but they were familiar. He had taken some in the past on the way to other places, on the way to friends or pubs. A long time ago.

He reached a fork in the road. The street on the left was familiar, it would take him past the shopping arcade. The street on the right wasn't familiar. So he took a right. And so he continued, taking turns he'd never taken or couldn't remember taking, until he was lost. Absolutely lost.

He parked his car, switched off the engine, closed his eyes and did nothing.

Then he opened his eyes and looked out the windows, to the left, to the right, and straight ahead, being careful not to accidentally look at the clock.

It was a council estate, by the looks of it. Across the road was a park. A big park. A swing park with rides and things to climb on, all made of metal that had been painted over a hundred times in red and green and yellow. Further away, behind the park, was a field. A field that would take ten minutes to run to the far side of. On the field were goalposts, broken.

He closed his eyes again, and a long time passed.

Just look at the time. Just look at the clock and look at the time.

He looked. It was 11.07. Sarah was probably telling them that he was running late but he'd be there in just a minute. At 11.15, she would probably send a text. And then at 11.20, there would be another text. And then at 11.30, there would be a phone call.

Then he would have to come back. He would have go back, because there was nowhere else for him to go. And the later he left it, the more questions there would be.

He should go now. Just go now. He could call Sarah as he was driving. She would hear that he was in the car, and it would make him sound like he was on his way, make him sound like there was nothing out of the ordinary and nothing to worry about.

He maybe just needed a holiday. He'd speak to him from downstairs. Gordon. Gordon said he'd come up next week and pay him a visit. Maybe he could book a holiday. Maybe if he chatted with Gordon about exactly what type of holiday he needed, Gordon would understand, being a boss himself.

Gordon's face was so pale for somebody who sold holidays.

Ben saw something move out the side of his eye, something out the right window, across the road. He looked, expecting to see a person, but it was a dog.

It was walking along the pavement on the opposite side of the road next to the park. It was by itself, and it was carrying something in its mouth. A ball. The ball was green, so it was probably a tennis ball. Probably a burst tennis ball.

Ben watched the dog as it trotted along. It was a mongrel. Sandy coloured. He couldn't tell what breeds went into making the dog, but whatever the blend was, it seemed to have resulted in the dog having one ear up and one ear down. The ears didn't look like something the dog could fix by giving its head a shake, it seemed permanent. As the dog bobbed along, the floppy ear flapped up and down, but the dog didn't seem to mind. It didn't seem to mind anything at all. It walked briskly, but not in a hurry. It didn't look rushed.

It didn't look harassed. It looked like it wanted to be wherever it wanted to be.

It had no collar, and Ben wondered if that meant it was a stray. He wondered how it got fed. It had no collar and there was no owner in sight. He worried about it, but the dog didn't seem to be worried about a thing. It turned to walk through the front gate of the park, and began walking towards the field, even though there was no one in the field or anything that Ben could see that would give it a reason to go there. The dog seemed to know what it was doing. Or maybe it didn't, but didn't care. It had its ball.

A memory came to Ben. He once saw a video on YouTube that compared the size of planets and stars and other things in the known universe, all laid out side by side. First you had the smaller planets of the solar system, like Earth. Next to that were bigger planets like Neptune. Then bigger, till Jupiter. Then the Sun, which was big next to Jupiter and enormous next to Earth. But then there were more. Stars that he had never heard of, dwarfing the Sun like the Sun dwarfed Earth. And then there were other stars that dwarfed those. Until you could barely get your head around the enormity of what you were looking at.

Next to that was the burst tennis ball in the dog's mouth.

Julie asked Sarah to send a text, just a gentle reminder, but there was no reply. She gave it five minutes then sent another, but there was still no reply. At 11.45, with the meeting kept waiting, Julie asked Sarah to give Ben a phone call. Ben answered, but it sounded like it was answered by accident. All she heard were strange talking sounds muffled through his pocket. Then the phone hung up.

Sarah walked into the boardroom, where Julie was waiting with the rest of the team. She told the team about the call, and the strange sounds.

'Strange sounds?' asked Julie. 'What like?'

Sarah said it sounded like a dog.

They laughed and asked Sarah what she meant. Was it an actual dog or did Ben sound like a dog? Sarah laughed and told them, no, it wasn't Ben sounding like a dog, it was an actual dog.

But, if she was being completely honest, she wasn't really sure.

Box Set

Aaron and Emily were watching a box set. They'd been watching it all week. Last night they finished at the second last episode, before Aaron said he had to go to bed because he was falling asleep. Emily had said she was going to stay up and watch something else. She wasn't tired.

Now it was the night after, and Aaron wanted to watch that last episode.

'D'you fancy sticking it on now?' asked Aaron, picking up the remote.

'What?' asked Emily.

'The last episode,' he said.

'Oh that. Aye, alright, if you want. Just a minute.'

'Are you watching this?' asked Aaron, looking at the documentary on the telly. 'Watch it if you want. I just thought you'd want to watch the last episode. I've been choking for it.'

Aaron loved it. The box set. Everything had been building up to this last episode. A lot of unanswered questions. He'd made sure he didn't mention on Twitter that he was watching it, in case anybody spoiled it out of badness.

'All right then,' she said. 'Stick it on.'

Aaron got up from the couch to switch a few of the lamps off. This last episode was a big deal. It was the end of the entire series. The series finale, as they say.

'Right,' he said, excited. 'Here it is.' And he sat down and pressed play.

And they watched.

And what a fucking episode it was.

Halfway through it, Aaron hit pause again, simply to turn to Emily and say, 'Seriously, what a fucking programme this is. D'you not think?'

'It's good,' said Emily, nodding.

The pair of them loved it. It was a dark comedy, that's how Aaron saw it. It was serious in parts with shocks and deaths and cruelty, but it was also funny. They'd go from laughing one minute, to sitting in stunned silence the next with their jaws hanging open, to laughing again, to then being almost in tears not long after. Aaron didn't know how they managed to write something like that, they were magicians.

He unpaused it and they continued to watch.

At around three-quarters through the episode, Aaron had a quick glance at his phone. He'd sometimes have a glance at Twitter during a quiet bit of an episode, when it seemed like nothing was happening. But Emily saw what he was doing and ticked him off.

'Don't,' she said. 'You'll miss this.'

Aaron looked at the telly, but he could see that he was missing nothing. The main character, Reno, was just walking across a car park. He wasn't with anybody, nothing was being said.

But then a car came from out of nowhere and ran him over.

'Jesus!' said Aaron.

The car drove off, leaving Reno lying there. He wasn't moving. There was no way he was going to be moving after that. He hadn't just been clipped by the side of the car, he had gone right over the top.

'Oh my God,' said Emily, with her hand over her mouth.

'That better not be it,' said Aaron.

'Shhhh,' said Emily.

'It better not be,' he said again. Had they killed Reno? Is that how this fucking thing ends? He looked at Emily. She looked as shocked as he was. 'Fucking hell,' he said.

The car came to a stop, and the door opened. You couldn't see who was in the motor, not yet.

But wait.

Wait a minute. Something wasn't right.

Aaron paused it. He paused it right there, and then he turned to Emily.

Emily pointed to the telly and said, 'What you doing? Press play.'

But he just looked at her.

'What?' she asked.

'How did you know?' he asked her.

'How did I know what?' she asked.

He looked at the telly, at Reno lying in the car park, and pointed at it.

'What?' she said. 'That? Him getting knocked down? I didn't. I didn't know.'

'But you said I was going to miss a bit.'

Emily looked at him like he was talking shite. 'Gonnae just press play, Aaron?' She reached for the remote. But he pulled it away.

'Did you watch it?' he asked. 'You watched it, didn't you?'

'No,' she said.

'Then why did you say that I was going to miss something? How did you know?'

'I didnae know,' she said. 'I just meant that you were gonnae miss the episode. You're looking at your phone and it's the last episode.'

Aaron was sure he'd looked at his phone at an earlier

part of the episode as well, but she'd said nothing then. Why was that? Why didn't she say he was going to miss something then? Why did she only say it before Reno got hit by a motor?

'Did you watch it?' he asked again. 'Tell the truth, Emily. I don't care.'

He did care.

She looked back at him for a moment, and then told the truth. She started laughing, then told him the truth.

'All right, I watched it,' she said. She took his hand and laughed again. 'I just wanted to watch it.'

'What?' he asked. 'What? Why did you do that?'

'Because I wisnae tired and I wanted something to watch.'

'The last episode,' said Aaron, pointing at the telly. 'You serious? You fucking serious?'

He was pissed off.

'Aaron, I wanted to watch it and you didnae. You went to bed. The final episode, and you decide to go to bed. Fair's fair. Anyway, it's just a fucking programme. Get a grip.'

Aaron thought that maybe she was right. Maybe he was blowing it out of proportion. It was just a programme.

But it wasn't just that, was it? There was something else. Something wasn't right about it. There was something bigger, but he couldn't put it into words just yet. So he took his hand away from hers, and looked at the telly, with the series still paused. He tried to figure it out.

'Go,' she said. 'Press play. It's good.'

He didn't like that. That was something there he didn't like. He didn't like hearing her saying that it was good, reminding him that she'd gone ahead without him.

Was he overreacting?

He looked back over his mind to see if he'd ever done the same thing to her. He probably had. In fact, he knew he had. He remembered that he finished watching a few episodes of *The Wire* once when she wanted to watch them with him.

But that was different.

It was different because she wasn't that interested in *The Wire*. He'd asked her night after night if she fancied watching those episodes, but she said no, preferring to watch something else. She said she wanted to watch them eventually, but she was in no rush, whereas he wanted to watch them right away.

But it wasn't just that.

He'd owned up. That was one difference here. He owned up the very next day. He told her the very next morning in bed, before they got up. He said sorry, but she didn't mind, and then he told her what had happened in the episodes that he'd watched. And as he was telling her, she cut him off, because she wasn't that interested after all. She didn't even know half the characters' names.

But it wasn't just that either. There was something bigger.

'Aaron, gonnae press play?' she said.

So he pressed play and pretended to be watching, when he was thinking more about this other thing. It was starting to come to him now, what was really wrong here.

While she had been watching this episode, before he found out that she'd already seen it, she had been pretending that she hadn't already seen it.

She had been laughing. She'd been laughing at things that she would surely no longer find funny, because she'd already seen it. When you see a funny thing for the second time, you don't laugh the way she had laughed.

She had opened her mouth in shock at things that she could not have found shocking, because she had already seen it. She looked right at him with surprise on her face, as he looked the same way back at her. He thought he was sharing an experience with her. And he hadn't been. And she knew that.

She had deceived him. And she was good at it.

Too good.

And what about the tears? The tears at that bit when Reno knew he wasn't getting his daughter back. Aaron had turned to Emily and pointed at his cheek to show her the tear rolling down it. And he saw that Emily was in tears as well.

Had she faked those tears?

Can you be in tears twice, at the same thing, two nights in a row? Surely you need time to let the memory clear from your mind in order to be upset again, for the grief to be new?

He wanted to ask her.

He paused the episode, and said 'Emily'. But then he said 'Forget it', and pressed play.

He couldn't put the questions into words. He didn't know what it was he wanted to ask, or if he wanted an answer.

How was she able to fake her emotions so convincingly? When, during their relationship, had she done it before? When would she do it again? Could she be truthful from this point on? If she said yes, how would he know if that was the truth?

They watched the rest of the episode, and Aaron pretended that what she did wasn't important, that it was nothing.

'Sorry for overreacting,' he said. But he didn't mean it. So in that respect, he was a bit like her.

But he wasn't. What she had done was different.

Six years later, her dad died. By that time, Aaron and Emily had split up, but Emily had invited him to the funeral, because he and her dad had got on well.

At the reception afterwards, Aaron was standing near Emily, as she was talking to one her uncles, one of her dad's brothers.

Aaron watched her as she wiped away her tears.

Emily saw him. Saw him looking at her. Looking closely at her face, from only a few feet away. Looking very closely.

Studying her.

'Don't, Aaron,' she said. 'Just fucking don't.'

Trainers

Yvonne went to the shops to buy a new pair of trainers for her son Paul. He was in primary 2, and there was going to be a race at the school. She wanted him to win, but he had no chance. He was too slow.

She took him to the shops and bought the trainers from one of the assistants. He was a strange person to be an assistant in a shoe shop. He was a very old man with a long beard. Everybody else in there was young.

Yvonne told the man that Paul was going to be in a race. Paul said that he never won, and he looked sad. But the old man smiled.

'Then perhaps you would like these trainers here, young man?'

The old man handed over a pair of trainers, the likes of which Yvonne had never seen before.

'These are special shoes, my fellow. Magic shoes. With these shoes, you will run faster than before. You will jump higher than before. You will run longer than before.'

'I don't need to jump,' said Paul. 'It's just a race going straight forward.'

Yvonne laughed, and so did the old man. He had an old man's laugh that went 'Haaa haaa haaaaaa'.

She asked the old man how much they cost, worried that they would break the bank, like all trainers these days. But he said to Paul, 'For you, my child, I give them to you for free.'

Yvonne said, 'I wish. But how much really?'

The old man said, 'I'm being quite genuine, my dear.'

So Yvonne thanked the man and so did Paul, and away they went.

Paul wanted to try the trainers on right away the second he left the shop. He said they were magic trainers. Yvonne went along with it and said yes, they're magic, but she didn't want him getting them all dirty right away.

They waited until later that day, and Yvonne took him to the park to try them out.

Yvonne said to Paul, 'On your marks. Get set. Go!'

And you had to see the speed of Paul. He was running fast as fuck. He wasn't running unnaturally fast, but a lot faster than usual.

They really were magic trainers.

'Oh my God,' said Yvonne. She knew that when it came to the race, her son was going to win. She couldn't wait, and neither could Paul.

On the morning of the race, a junkie stole Paul's trainers.

What happened was, Yvonne had walked Paul around to school wearing his normal shoes, so that the magic trainers didn't get dirty. Then when they got there, she took the magic trainers out of her bag and put them on the wall at the school fence, while she took the normal shoes off Paul's feet. And that's how quickly it happened. A junkie was off with them, just like that.

Paul was heartbroken.

'I'm never going to win now,' he said. 'Never. Not without my magic trainers.'

Yvonne said, 'Wait here.' And she drove back to the shop to try and buy another pair.

When she got there, she asked around for the old man, but none of the staff knew who she was talking about. Was there something they could help her with? Yvonne told them she was after a pair of trainers, a specific pair of trainers, and she described the ones she was after. They didn't know what trainers she was talking about. They couldn't help.

Yvonne picked out a pair, the cheapest she could find, which weren't that cheap at all. They looked dreadful. All purple and black with green bits. Nothing like the magic ones.

She rushed back to school and got to Paul just before the race. She showed him the trainers she got, and he burst into tears.

'I know, sweetheart,' she said. 'I know, they don't look good. But the old man told me that they're even more magic than the ones before.'

Paul looked up to her, wiping his tears.

'Really?'

'Really,' said Yvonne. 'They're the most magic ones in the world.'

Paul began to smile, and looked at the trainers with new eyes. Then Yvonne helped him put them on.

She felt seriously bad. She knew that Paul was going to come last, then he'd know they weren't really magic.

Paul took his place at the start of the race, and Yvonne watched on, her hands almost covering her eyes. She didn't want to look.

The head teacher shouted, 'On your marks. Get set. Go!'

And off they ran.

Yvonne closed her eyes until she heard the cheer at the end. She opened them, and expected to see Paul not even past the finish line.

But guess who had won?

That's right.

Paul.

He ran fast as fuck, and he won.

Yvonne gave Paul a big cuddle, and he told her that he loved his new trainers even more. He said they were the most magic trainers in the whole world. Even though they weren't.

Which just goes to show you.

If you believe. If you believe and you have a dream, and you think you can do it, and you want to do it, you can do it. You can do anything you put your mind to. Anything you set your heart on.

It goes to show you that all your dreams can and will come true. The magic isn't in the trainers, but within each and every one of us.

They caught the junkie and gave him 18 months.

Throw away the key, that's what I say.

The Tree

Billy woke up one morning and there it was. A tree, no more than two inches high, growing out of his shoulder.

He tried pulling it off, but to no avail. This wasn't some young sapling he could pluck out like it was a blade of grass, this was the chunky and ancient type that looked like it had been there for hundreds of years, rooted to the spot.

It would take a bit of work getting rid of it, but he knew he could do it. He'd just get a saw, and then dig out the stump with a teaspoon or fork. He'd have to make sure the council didn't find out about it, though, as they probably wouldn't give him permission. He knew somebody who had a bird's nest in his roof, wrecking his roof, and the council wouldn't let him get rid of it.

He showed his wife and son the tree and told them not to tell anybody, in case the council got wind of it, but he may as well have shouted it over a megaphone. By the end of the day, there were neighbours and youngsters queuing at the front door to get a gander.

A wee lassie pointed at the tree, telling her mum that she liked the wee boys playing on the swing. Billy thought it was just her imagination, but when he looked, sure enough, miniature boys about a millimetre high had tied a length of rope around one of the branches and were daring each other to swing higher.

Billy shook his head and sighed. Everybody knew about the tree now, everybody from normal-sized people to the boys swinging on the tree. It was only a matter of time before the council knew about it as well.

He hoped that maybe people would lose interest in the tree, which would cause them to stop talking about it, which would help reduce the chances of word getting to the council. But then he opened the door one morning, and there on the doorstep were people from the news. People from the papers and the telly.

There were reporters that he recognised from break-fast telly pointing a camera in his face before he'd even had a chance to wake up. They were smiling and asking how it felt to have this tree growing out his shoulder, he must be bowled over with all the attention he was getting.

He said he was sick of it and he was going to chop it down.

He regretted saying that on national telly, because, surprise surprise, within an hour of saying it, a guy from the council was at the door to tell Billy he wasn't allowed. The tree and the surrounding shoulder was now a conservation area, or some other bureaucratic claptrap like that. The council guy laid on the guilt trip about helping wildlife and preserving green spaces for future generations.

But the guy from the council wasn't the one that had to put up with having a tree on his shoulder. He wasn't the one being kept awake, night and fucking day, with the wee boys playing on that swing. Or the underage drinkers that would come out at night, covering his shoulder with broken bottles and sick. Or the wee miniature couples that would come and shag under the tree, just as he was about to read his weans a bedtime story.

So Billy set the fuck about it with an axe.

He popped open his son's box of toys, grabbed the axe off the Lego lumberjack and just set the fuck about it.

His son saw him, and screamed. His wife ran in. A miniature guy who'd been shagging under the tree made a run for it, but tripped over the trousers that were down around his ankles and fell to his death, splatting onto a Dr Seuss book below.

When Billy's wife and son tried to take the axe off him, he took the axe to them as well, chopping them into tiny wee pieces. It took fucking ages, but he did it, before turning the axe on himself. Which took even longer.

And so he was buried with his wife and son. Dead and buried.

Good, that's the end of that.

Except it wasn't. Nothing's easy in this life, didn't you know?

Because the next day, sprouting from their grave, was a tree.

It was the chunky and ancient type that looked like it had been there for a hundred years. And there, growing out one of the branches, was Billy, no more than two inches high, rooted to the spot from the waist up, next to his wife and son.

And they remembered exactly what he did. Oh, how they remembered.

He sometimes wished for a bird to land nearby and mistake him for a worm. He wished for a bird to pull his fucking head off and put him out of his misery.

Or for a slug to slither over the lot of them, or maybe just the other two, to give his fucking ears a rest, even if for just five minutes.

Or simply just to be crushed by a falling chestnut. Was that too much to ask?

But that's not how things were going to go. Because here, coming his way, was a caterpillar. A big, hungry caterpillar. A caterpillar that would munch him up one bite at a time, with that big, horrible mouth.

He wondered if he'd wake up again, after he died, to find himself sticking out the shoulder of a butterfly, the butterfly that this caterpillar would turn into.

That would be nice. He'd prefer to just die and never wake up, but if this was going to go on and on, then that would be a nice break. Riding on top of a butter-fly, a beautiful butterfly, fluttering around in the sunshine, carried around in the warm summer air – providing he was away from the other two.

It would be good if he was up at the butterfly's shoulder, and the other two were far away at the other end, down at its arse. That would be nice.

But then, of course, the butterfly would be caught and stuck in a jar, what with it being beautiful and everything.

He'd spend his last few hours in the sweltering heat of an empty jam jar lying in the sun, attached to a panicked butterfly battering itself off an invisible glass wall.

Or worse, whoever caught the butterfly might see him on its shoulder. They might torture him, the way wee boys pull the wings off flies.

He couldn't believe this was happening. How things had turned out.

So if you ever see a tree growing out your shoulder, or anything like that, don't tell anybody. Just get rid of the thing. And especially don't tell the council.

They care more about trees than they care about people.

The Daysnatcher

Sean and Kim were sitting outside a pub, in the sunshine. Kim was leaning her head back with her eyes closed, to get some colour in her face.

'Some heat, in't it?' she asked Sean.

Sean didn't answer.

Kim opened her eyes to see why he wasn't answering, and she saw that he wasn't listening. He looked distant.

'What are you thinking?' she asked.

He didn't answer. His eyes were looking downward, then they moved to the side, as he thought about whatever he was thinking. His brow furrowed, then it relaxed.

Kim had to ask again. 'Hellooooo,' she said, waving her hand in front of his face.

Sean looked at her. 'Sorry, what?'

'I said, what are you thinking? Are you all right?'

Sean put a hand on his drink. 'I was just thinking ...', then he shook his head.

'What?' asked Kim. She spoke more gently. 'Your mum?'

'No,' said Sean. 'No.'

He moved in his chair and raised his hands to try and help him word what he was about to say. He said, 'I was just wondering where the days go.'

Kim nodded and looked around at the people walking by. She looked at a lassie across the road who was about ten years younger than herself, and said, 'I know. Time flies.'

'No,' said Sean. 'I don't mean like that.'

She looked at him.

He tapped his right temple and said, 'I mean the days in here.'

Kim thought for a second, then shook her head. 'Hmm?'

She took a sip of her Diet Coke. She wasn't thirsty. She was just trying to appear relaxed and not concerned about him. He'd told her before to stop worrying about him, but it was hard not to. Especially when he tapped his head.

'I mean, where do they go?' he said. 'But I don't mean the days you remember. I mean the ones you don't. Where do they go?'

'I don't know what you're getting at,' said Kim. 'You mean the days you forget? Are you asking what happens when you forget?' She shrugged. 'I don't know. You just … forget.'

She laughed, but she tried not to sound like she was laughing at him. 'Simple as that, I suppose.'

'I don't know,' said Sean, not content with the answer. 'I'm not sure.' Then he had a sip of his own drink.

Kim was going to end the conversation there. She wasn't sure if it was good for Sean to get into all of this. But maybe it was a good thing. She didn't know. But she decided to ask.

'What kind of things were you thinking?' she said. 'Things like what?'

He moved his seat to face her. He'd been facing out towards the road, but now he turned his seat so that he could lean forward towards her to say what was on his mind.

'I was just trying to think of happy memories,' he said. 'Happier times. Like, have I ever said to you that my favourite time was when I was eight?'

'Eight,' said Kim. 'Aye. You've mentioned it a few times.'

She had another sip of her drink.

'Well,' said Sean. 'I've been thinking about it, and I cannae actually remember it.'

She put down her drink and shrugged. 'Well, it was a long time ago. I cannae remember being eight.'

'I know,' said Sean. Then he pointed to himself. 'But I can.'

He saw that she was confused.

'What I mean is, what I mean is, I thought I did. I thought I remembered it. I had it in my head that it was one of the happiest times of my life. I always go on about it, don't I? I know I do.'

Kim looked away. 'It's fine, though,' she said. 'There's nothing wrong with happy memories. You should cherish your memories.'

'Aye, but.' He shook his head. 'But. When I go to try and remember things, all the good things that happened, I can only remember one or two things. And I mean that. Just one or two things.'

He tapped on the table with the edge of his hand to emphasise. 'Literally *one* or *two things*.'

Kim looked at his hand.

He smiled and said, 'You'd think that I'd remember more, win't you? Considering it was supposed to be the happiest time of my life, considering I go on about it so much. Yet when I try to remember, all I get in my head is just one or two things, and that's it. That's the lot, Kim. I mean it.'

'Well,' she said. 'The main thing is that you remember that it was a happy time. I think that's the main thing.'

'But was it?' asked Sean. 'Was it a happy time? I can only remember, like, two things. Honestly. I was thinking about it there, that's what I was thinking about. I asked myself, right, see what you can remember. Go. See what you can remember. And all I could remember was this …'

He counted on his fingers. One: 'A fence that I used to vault when me and my mum went to Saltcoats.' Two: 'The weather was nice.'

He opened out his empty palms to show that there was nothing else there.

Kim said, 'Sean, it's the same for everybody. I cannae remember being eight.' She laughed. 'I'm not even sure if I can remember what happened eight weeks ago!'

'But Kim! I need … you don't have the … it isn't the …'

She waited for him to calm down. He usually did.

He took a breath and looked away. 'There's got to be more than that.'

He lifted his glass to take a drink, then stopped halfway to put it back down on the table to talk some more. 'Look,' he said, calmly. 'Look, right. It's like this. I'm sorry, by the way, I'm just …'

'It's fine,' she said. 'Go.'

He took another breath.

'It's like. It's as if. Imagine you've got all this money in the bank, right?'

'Right,' she said. She put a hand on her drink.

'Imagine you've got all this money that you've been saving up. Saving up for years. Saving for a rainy day, right?'

She nodded.

'But then,' he said, 'you go to check your account one day. Maybe you need to take some of it out, I don't know. And you look. And it's gone. Somebody's snatched it. It's all gone.'

'It's not all gone.'

'All right, maybe not all gone. But all you've got left is just a wee pile of change. A wee pile of coppers. A wee pile of manky fucking two-pence pieces, a wee pile of twos and ones that you don't want.'

She smiled, she thought he was being funny. But he didn't smile back.

'Sean, I think that's quite a negative way of looking at it.' She leaned forward. 'I cannae remember everything about being eight, nobody can.'

'It's not just that,' said Sean. He opened his mouth to speak, then closed it.

'I know,' said Kim. 'I know.' She leaned forward to take his hand. 'But you don't have to remember every single thing to have happy memories.'

Sean looked at her, then looked down the street over her shoulder. She thought he was thinking, but Kim could tell from his eyes that he was looking at something. He began to smile, so she turned to see what he was smiling at.

There was an old woman in the distance, walking along the pavement in their direction. She was pushing a tartan shopping trolley in front of her. It looked like it was also helping her walk, like a Zimmer frame.

Kim watched Sean watching the woman. He said nothing for a while, then he spoke.

'I'm not being negative,' he said, looking in the direction of the woman. 'I'm not. In fact, it's funny.'

He laughed a wee laugh. Kim smiled, but not fully, as she waited to see what kind of laugh he was laughing.

'It is funny,' he said, still watching the woman. 'You check your account, thinking it'll be stacked with all these gold bars. All these happy memories. All these memories of all these happy days you're sure you had. And they've been snatched.' He pointed to the woman in the distance and said, 'Snatched by her.'

Kim turned around to look at the woman, then she turned back to Sean.

She laughed politely, but she didn't think it was funny.

She watched him as he watched the woman. His eyes moved down then up again, looking between the woman's face and her trolley and everything in between.

'The Daysnatcher,' he said to himself.

He looked at Kim. She was looking at him, but with her head turned slightly towards the old woman behind, listening. She knew the woman was close, because of the squeak coming from one of the wheels on the trolley.

'Imagine it,' said Sean. 'Imagine such a thing.'

'It's funny,' said Kim.

'Aye,' said Sean. 'And I widnae mind. Now that I think about it, I really widnae. I really don't. I had good days, I know I did.'

'Of course you did. You widnae have they feelings if you didnae.'

'Aye,' he said. 'So I don't mind if she wants to snatch a few. Take a few of the good memories for herself. And I'm not judging, maybe she needs them more than me!'

Kim nodded.

'It's just,' he said. 'I don't know.'

Kim finished for him. 'You just wish she'd take some of the bad ones as well.'

Sean looked at her and nodded. 'I just wish she would take some of the bad ones as well.' He laughed another wee laugh. They both laughed.

The old woman began to pass. She glanced at Sean and saw him looking at her. She smiled at him, and he smiled back.

Sean turned his smile onto Kim. He said again, 'I just wish she would take some of the bad ones.'

Kim had another sip of her Diet Coke, until it was finished.

Sean faced her, but with his head turned slightly towards the old woman behind. He listened to her squeaky wheel fade away.

He turned to look at the woman, to see where she was. She was far away. He shouted, 'I just wish she would take some of the ...'

Kim grabbed his arm to turn him back towards her.

Soft Play

Claire and Tom were sitting at a table in a soft play. Their daughters were running around somewhere with the other boys and lassies, playing out of sight for most of the time. They'd sometimes shout hello to their mum and dad from high up in the multi-coloured scaffolding, or come back to the table for a quick drink before running off again, but they'd mostly stay away. It was a chance for Claire and Tom to chat in peace, if they wanted to, but they sat there without saying much.

Tom was bored. He had his side turned to Claire, as he looked at a polystyrene cup of coffee on the table that somebody had left behind. He was moving the coffee inside the cup, simply by using the power of his mind. It was just something he did when he got bored. Claire looked at the coffee inside the cup as it moved around.

She didn't like it.

Claire was about to interrupt him, when she spotted a woman that she knew, called Diane. Claire knew Diane from a class that they used to take their children to. All the mums would sit around in a circle with their babies, bouncing them up and down to music. While the dads were off doing something more fun. Something less boring.

'Diane!' shouted Claire.

Diane turned and saw her, and over she came to the table. 'Claire,' she said. 'How are you? Long time no see.'

Diane gave Claire a cuddle and asked how she was doing. She looked to Tom and was about to say hi to him as well, but she could see that he was in a world of his own.

'Oh, forget about him,' said Claire. She said it with a smile, to pretend that it didn't bother her as much as it did. 'How you getting on? How's Patrick?'

The last time Claire had seen Diane, she was with her son Patrick. Diane had mentioned that Patrick was going for a hearing test, because something was flagged up after a routine check-up at the doctor's.

'He's good,' said Diane, looking towards the scaffolding. 'He's in there somewhere. How are yours, how are the twins?'

'Good, good,' said Claire. 'Hard work, but I'm coping. Oh, how did things go with Patrick's hearing? I remember you saying he was going for a test.'

'Ear wax. That's all it was.'

'Really? You'd have thought they would have saw that at the check-up.'

'Mmm-hmm.'

Diane looked at what Tom was doing with the coffee in the cup.

Claire followed her eyes and saw what she was looking at.

'Hmm,' said Claire. 'This.'

Both of them watched what he was doing. He was doing something over and over.

The coffee would start off looking like a normal cup of coffee, with the surface of the coffee being flat and horizontal. Then the coffee would slowly rise at one side of the cup, like the cup was being tipped, except the cup was flat on the table.

Then, as the coffee started to reach the lip of the cup, it would suddenly drop back down inside, as if whatever force that was causing the coffee to rise had been suddenly switched off. The surface of the coffee would rock back and forth until it came to a rest.

After a few seconds of it sitting at rest, it would begin to rise again like before.

'You're going to spill it,' said Claire.

She was annoyed. She tried not to let it show to Diane, but she was annoyed.

What annoyed her wasn't that he was about to spill the coffee. It was that he was able to move stuff with his mind, and she wasn't. Not that she was jealous of being able to do it, it wasn't that either.

She'd like to be able to, though. She would. She'd love to.

She'd tried it herself, in the past. She was sure that most people had tried it when they were bored. She tried it when she was younger, tried moving things just by looking at them. She'd be stuck in the house with her dad after being grounded, stuck in the living room with the telly off, with nothing to look at, nothing to read. And faced with that level of boredom, her mind would have no choice but to occupy itself with daft things to think about, like wondering if she could move something with her mind. She'd look at an ashtray or something else lying around, and give it a go, just to see if she could. But, of course, she couldn't.

Tom could, though.

He would never say how, but he didn't have to. Claire had worked it out. It was because in order to be able to do it, you couldn't just be bored. You couldn't just be the type of bored you get when there's nothing to watch on the telly. You had to be a special type of bored. The type of bored you get when you're stuck in a soft play with no connection on your phone, stuck with a family that you're bored of. Stuck with a life that you're bored of.

What, and she wasn't? Did he think that she wasn't also bored?

Claire and Diane continued to watch what Tom was doing with the cup of coffee. It was now floating above the table by a centimetre or so. There was a shadow underneath.

'Mum,' said a voice.

Claire looked and saw it was Diane's son Patrick, who was walking over with his jacket on.

'Well just look at you!' said Claire.

He'd grown. He was the same age and height as Claire's daughter, but the last time she'd seen Patrick, he was no more than a baby. Now he was a walking, talking boy.

Patrick didn't respond, he was more interested in what Tom was doing.

'Look!' said Patrick, pointing to the cup.

The cup was now upside down, in mid-air, with the coffee spiralling around the outside like a helter-skelter.

'Do you like it?' asked Claire. 'Can your daddy do that?'

'No,' said Patrick.

No, of course he can't, Patrick. That's because he isn't bored with his life. He isn't bored with his family. He isn't bored with your mum.

And even if he is, he doesn't let everybody know about it by doing shite like this.

Claire hoped Diane wouldn't say something to make her feel better, something like 'Oh, Tom's good at that, isn't he, Patrick?'

Claire just wanted her to go.

The New Icon

There once was this guy called Malcolm.

Malcolm had a company that made apps. Apps for phones and tablets. Some of them were games, and some of them were apps that he thought people would find useful. But they were all shite. They were all flops. Each of them only had about 400 downloads and they weren't rated very highly, no more than 3 out of 5 stars. People would leave comments under the ratings, saying that the apps were a waste of time, and that other apps did more stuff and did it better. The comments and ratings for the games were just as bad, with people saying the games were just rip-offs of *Candy Crush* and *Angry Birds*. They were all flops, each and every one of them.

Well, except one.

There was one that wasn't a flop. It was quite a success. It was called YoonifEye, pronounced 'Unify'. It sort of unified all your social-media stuff, like Twitter and Facebook and things like that. It brought them all together. It unified them.

The app was very popular, it had just under a million downloads, and an average rating of 4.5 out of 5. The free version was ad supported, with the ad-free version costing £2.99. It brought in a good income for Malcolm's company, MalcolmApps, which helped him to employ a small team of five people. Nobody in his position would have any reason to go and fuck with a success like that. YoonifEye looked good, it worked good, everybody liked it, there was no reason to change a thing. There was just no reason to change it at all.

Malcolm decided that he wanted to change it.

Despite everybody liking it the way it was, despite everything else being a failure and this one app being a success, he wanted to change it.

He called a Monday morning meeting, and told his staff that he'd been using the app over the weekend. He wanted to make a very small change. 'It's nothing, really,' he said. 'I'm getting a bit bored of the icon. The app icon.' Then he clapped his hands and rubbed them together. 'I think it's time for a change!' He was all excited.

He was a fucking fool.

'What's wrong with it?' asked Jen, the designer. It was her that designed the original icon, the current

icon. It was a fair question, because there was absolutely fuck-all wrong with it. The icon was kind of like
an eye, because of the word 'Eye' in 'YoonifEye', but
the eye spiralled into the centre, like it was taking all
these things from around, and spiralling it together. To
unify them. D'you get it?

I think that's quite clever.

Now why would you want to go and change
that?

'I'm not looking for any major changes,' said
Malcolm, raising his hand, smiling. 'Don't worry, nothing major. I just think it's time to freshen it up a bit,
and I'm sure a lot of users would agree.'

I'm sure a lot of users wouldn't have agreed. I'm sure
a lot of users didn't give a fuck. Everything was fine.
Just leave it the way it is, Malcolm.

'All right,' said Jen, shrugging. 'Just to let you know,
I don't think it needs freshening up. But you're the
boss.'

Malcolm nodded.

'So,' said Jen. 'What is it you're thinking?'

'I'm thinking …' said Malcolm, drumming
his fingers on his chin. 'I'm thinking of something
that's the same as what we've got just now. But
different.'

'You're wanting the same,' repeated Jen. 'But different.' Maybe if Malcolm heard back what he just said,

he'd know how much of a clown he was. She opened up her notepad. 'The same,' she said as she scribbled it down. 'But different.'

And then she did a full stop. Tap.

'Great,' said Malcolm. 'Let me see what you've done before lunch. Midday, shall we say?'

'If you want,' said Jen.

If he wants. Ha, that's a laugh. The cunt doesn't know *what* he wants. There was fuck-all wrong with that icon. Fuck-all.

But Jen went away and did what she could, making up a few different icons. Slightly different designs, but not too different, as per Malcolm's wishes. His stupid fucking wishes.

Midday came, and over walked Malcolm with a cup of coffee. He grabbed a seat, sat on it, and wheeled up next to Jen using his feet.

'Hey, Jen,' he said. 'Let's see what you've got.'

Jen showed Malcolm her ideas. They were just what he asked for. They were kind of the same as the current icon, but slightly different. Same but different. That's what he asked for.

'Hmmm,' he said, looking around the screen. 'Hmmm.'

'What d'you think?' asked Jen, not giving a fuck.

'Hmmm', said Malcolm. 'They're a bit too like what we've got.'

'Are you saying they're not different enough? You want them to be a bit more different?'

'That's exactly it,' said Malcolm, nodding. 'That's exactly it, I think they need to be a bit more different. Otherwise, what's the point? You know?'

'Yes,' said Jen.

Fuck off, Malcolm.

'Will I leave it with you then?' he said.

'Leave it with me.'

'Shall we reconvene at close of play?'

'Okay,' she said, and Malcolm left.

Close of play. Fuck off with that patter.

But she got to work, designing more icons, this time trying to make them a bit more different than the ones she'd already done, whilst still keeping them the same as what she'd already done. She had to stretch her neck a few times and go for a walk around the office, to try and get her head around it. To try and work out what the fuck he wanted. What the fuck was he on about?

She worked on till 6 p.m., until Malcolm headed over once again, sitting on an empty seat and then wheeling himself over by the feet until he was next to Jen. You know, instead of just pulling the seat over first and then sitting on it.

'Okay,' said Malcolm. 'Hit me with it.'

I'd love to hit you with it, mate. This was a total waste of time. There was fuck-all wrong with that icon.

Jen showed Malcolm what she'd been doing. She had twice as many variations as she had before, at least 20 new icon designs. There would be something in there for him.

She zoomed in to show each of them individually on the screen. Then, after a few seconds, she dragged over to the next design.

'Hmmm,' said Malcolm.

Oh fuck off with that hmmm shite.

'What d'you think?' asked Jen, rubbing her eyes. She was getting tired. Malcolm said nothing, so she kept dragging through all the icons until she had shown him them all.

'Hmmm,' he said.

'What?'

She didn't normally just say something as blunt as 'What?' to her boss, but she was knackered.

'You're going to hate me for saying this,' he said. 'But I think they're a bit too different.'

Oh my God. You tool.

'You think these ones are too different?' asked Jen.

'That's exactly it,' he said, nodding, smiling apologetically. 'I think we've departed too much from the current icon, I'm afraid. We don't want to lose that familiarity with the users.'

Then here's a fucking idea. How's about not changing the icon, mate? How's about not changing a thing? It's the only successful app you've made, it's got an average of 4.5 stars out of 5 and almost a million fucking downloads. Why not just leave it the way it is? How's that for an idea? What is it with people like you?

'Okay,' said Jen, sighing. She sighed the biggest fucking sigh you've ever heard in your life. 'Okay, well, I'll pick it up tomorrow.'

'No,' said Malcolm.

'What?' asked Jen, turning to look at him.

'I want this going live tonight,' he said, all excited again. 'Or tomorrow morning at the latest. Fraser's staying late to upload it, once you work your magic.'

'But ...' she said. She closed her eyes and put her hand to her brow. She didn't know what to say, she truly was knackered.

'I'll pay you overtime, don't worry about that. I'm just really excited about the users getting up tomorrow morning and seeing the new icon.'

Get a fucking life, mate. Seriously.

'All right,' said Jen.

So she stayed late, working till 8 p.m. to knock up more icons. She tried something that was a bit more like what they already had, but not too like what they already had. She didn't want him going 'Hmmm' and saying they weren't different enough again. But when he wheeled up to have a look, that's exactly what he said.

So she stayed till 11 p.m., knocking up even more, this time doing icons that were more different, but not too different. She threw in the odd icon that was completely different, just in case. Just in case of the unlikely event that he said, 'Oh, wait, I like that.' But when he wheeled over, it was the same 'Hmmm' patter. He pointed at the ones that were completely different and said 'Oh, those ones there', which made Jen hopeful that he'd seen something he liked and she was going to be able to get the fuck out of there. But no. 'Those ones there are far too different, that's not what I'm after at all,' he said.

He asked her to have one last crack at it. She told him that she was fucking shattered, she told him that she wasn't at her best. Her eyes were blurry and she was half asleep. She told him that she should really just go home and do it in the morning and they should update the icon another time. But he said no.

Keep that in mind. She warned him, right? She warned him. You can't blame her for what happened next.

At 3 a.m., Malcolm and Fraser came over to Jen's desk to see the designs. They were the only ones left in the office. Everybody else was tucked up in bed, where Jen wanted to be. Where she *should* have been.

She showed Malcolm the designs.

'Hmmm,' he said, shaking his head slowly. 'No. No, these aren't what I was after at all.'

Then you fucking do it, Malcolm. Better still, just don't do anything. Just leave it. The app has got an average of 4.5 out of 5 stars. Barely any app gets higher than that.

Malcolm was about to let it go. Maybe Jen was right and it was all a bit too rushed. He was just about to tell them to call the whole thing off, when he saw the last icon on the screen.

'Wait!' he said. 'That one. That one right there!'

Jen looked to see which one he was pointing at. It was one of the more different ones she did, it was quite a weird one. She couldn't even remember doing it. She was practically dreaming when she did it. At the time she was just thinking of the nonsense of doing something that was the same but different, the same but different, the same … but different. Then she nodded off. Then when she jumped back awake in her seat, there it was.

The icon was different from the rest. The other ones were static, they were pictures. Whereas this other one was animated. It was moving.

It was alive.

'I didn't know you could do that,' said Malcolm.

'You can't,' said Jen.

'You can't?' asked Malcolm.

'I don't know,' said Jen. She yawned and stretched, then shrugged. 'I don't know. All I know is that I'm really fucking tired.'

Malcolm and Fraser leaned in towards the screen for a closer look. As they leaned in, they could hear something.

'Can you hear that?' asked Malcolm.

'I can,' said Fraser. 'I can hear something.'

There was a metallic, breathing sound coming from the icon. It didn't sound like the in-out, in-out breathing that came from lungs, but a constant inhalation, drawing breath from where Jen, Malcolm and Fraser were sitting, into where the icon was. Wherever that was.

The spiral seemed to be spiralling like a whirlwind, yet it didn't seem to be moving at all. When you moved your head from side to side, you could see that the spiral was going into the screen. Deep beyond the screen. There was perspective.

The eye in the icon wasn't there anymore, except it somehow was. You could see it in your head, but you knew it wasn't really there on the screen. It was like each of them was simultaneously imagining seeing it there, without trying to imagine it.

And there was something bad about it. Something evil. There was the sense that it wanted to get you.

That would have set off the alarm bells for most people. But not Malcolm.

'I love it,' he said. 'I think it really stands out. Fraser, could you get that uploaded?'

'I'm not sure,' said Fraser. 'I don't think it'll work on Android. Besides, I don't think we should. There's something about it I don't like. I think it wants to get me.'

'Well, I love it,' said Malcolm. 'I think it's got an edge.'

He asked Fraser to upload it. Despite two warnings from his staff. Despite a warning from Fraser as well as that warning earlier from Jen. You can't pin this one on them.

'As for you, young lady,' he said, patting Jen on the back. 'Get to your bed. Good job.'

Malcolm headed home in his car and Jen got a taxi, while Fraser uploaded the updated app with the updated icon. He was going to test it, but it was so fucking late. It was after 3 in the morning. And keep in mind that it was Malcolm who kept them up that late. It was his fault, all this. There was nothing wrong with that icon. The original one, I mean.

The next morning, Malcolm strolled into the office, bright eyed and bushy tailed, saying good morning to the cleaning women. He was all excited about the new icon for YoonifEye. All excited to hear about the feedback from the users.

The team were crowded around Fraser's computer. Lying next to the desk was Maureen, one of the cleaners. She was lying face down in a pool of blood. Except her face itself wasn't face down, because her head was turned all the way around to face the ceiling.

'What's going on here then?' asked Malcolm, giving Maureen a nudge with his foot.

'We had a bit of a problem,' said Fraser.

'Problem? What problem?'

'I'll show you,' said Fraser. He looked to another one of the cleaning ladies. 'Agnes,' he said. 'Could you come over here for a minute?'

Agnes came over with a bin liner full of rubbish that she'd emptied from the bins next to the desks.

'Yes, pet?' she said, stepping over Maureen.

Fraser handed his phone over to Agnes. 'Could you press that button right there?' He pointed to the new icon for YoonifEye.

'Which one, love, this one here?'

'No, the one next to it, the one on the far left.'

'The one with the eye?' she asked.

'That's it,' said Fraser.

'Okay.' She looked at the icon, how it animated, and how it looked alive. She was impressed. 'Look at that, that's good.'

Malcolm smiled at Jen. Good feedback. Good feed-back so far.

Agnes hovered her finger over the button. Fraser pushed Malcolm back gently with his arm, to give Agnes a bit of room. Jen wheeled her seat away by a few feet.

Agnes tapped the button.

On tapping the button, she froze. She became as still as a waxwork. Then her head flicked to the side with such force and speed that it broke her neck. The sound of the crack gave Malcolm a fright. Her head flicked back the other way so quickly that you couldn't see it move. At one instant it was leaning to the right, and the very next instant it was leaning to the left, with no motion in between.

'And then watch her eye,' said Fraser.

Malcolm waited for something to happen. He was about to ask Fraser what he was supposed to be look-ing for, but then her left eye popped out, and hung from its nerve.

Malcolm looked to Fraser and Jen. He was concerned. He looked at their faces for answers, for solutions to this problem they'd got themselves into, but all they did was shrug. They shrugged because it wasn't them that got them into this problem. It was Malcolm's idea to keep them up till 3, despite Jen warning him. Fraser had warned him as well, he'd warned Malcolm that there wasn't enough time to test the icon. Remember Malcolm asked him to upload it without testing, and Fraser said 'I don't think we should'? Remember?

Malcolm was about to speak, but Fraser raised a finger to ask him to wait. Fraser looked at Agnes, as she stood there with her broken neck and popped-out eye. He waited a few seconds more, and said, 'Then this happens.' He pointed to Agnes.

A large purple vein began to swell on the right side of Agnes's face, opposite the side that had lost its eye. There was a creaking sound, like somebody twisting an old leather belt. Suddenly, the front of her body imploded. Her torso looked like an empty packet of crisps that had just had the air sucked out of it by a hoover.

Her head twisted to face behind her, quick enough to make her long grey hair flick Malcolm in the face. She fell forward next to her colleague Maureen. Body down, face up.

'I see,' said Malcolm. 'And it's not just an Android thing?'

'No,' said Fraser. 'That's Android and iOS. That's on everything.'

Well done Malcolm.

He could have just left it. There was absolutely fuck-all wrong with the icon the way it was. He could have just left it. It was a cracking wee app, with just under a million downloads, and an average rating of 4.5 out of 5 stars.

Well, guess what it is now.

3.9.

The Pub

The pub was shut. There was graffiti on it, and one of the windows at the front was smashed. The doorway had been boarded over, but it had been pulled away at the bottom. Above the doorway were letters that used to spell the name of the pub, but were now either broken or hanging upside down. The building was surrounded by a flimsy metal fence to keep people out, but it had been knocked over at the side of the pub, near the back.

A woman walked past the pub, carrying two poly bags of shopping. She raised one of the bags to her head, to wipe the sweat from her forehead with her hand. It was hot. A man walked her way. He was older than her, and he was drunk. He swayed from side to side. When he saw the woman, he straightened his back and looked ahead, to the horizon, and attempted to walk in a straight line. When he passed her, he returned to how he was.

He stopped to look at the pub, at the broken sign and the broken window. He looked around him. When he saw that there was nobody there, he spat on the ground in front of the fence. He began walking again.

There was a sign on the fence. He stopped, and walked backwards to look at it. The sign displayed the name of a construction company. He frowned, and looked at the pub again. He began walking away while he looked at the pub and the sign. He saw that the fence had been knocked over at the side of the building. He continued to walk, not looking where he was going. He stumbled over a stone. He tried to kick it away, but missed.

He began walking again, then he stopped. He looked back to the fence at the side of the building, where it had been knocked over. He looked through the fence at the front, and saw the gap at the bottom of the boarded-up doorway.

He looked to where the woman had been, the one that he'd passed, but she was far away down the street. There was nobody else in that direction. He looked around, and there was nobody else anywhere. He looked again at the sign on the fence, and then he began walking down the side of the pub, towards where the fence had been knocked over.

He stepped over the fence, and walked back towards the front of the pub. When he began to get closer to the front corner, he walked slower, and then stopped. He put a hand on one of the pillars at the front of the pub, and peered around it. He looked down the street to where the woman had gone, and saw that there was nobody there. He looked the other way. He looked behind him. Nobody was anywhere. He looked at his hand on the pillar. He ran his hand down it slowly. When his hand reached as far as it would go, he kept it there, and he looked at the pillar.

He walked around to the boarded-up doorway, and leaned over to grab it at the bottom. It was nailed at the top, but he was able to pull the bottom back far enough to make a large gap. He let go of the board and it slammed back against the frame. He looked down the street to see if anybody had heard the noise, but nobody was there. There was somebody far away where the woman had gone, but they were crossing the road and not coming his way. He got down on his knees and pulled the board back, and crawled through the gap that he'd made.

He stood up inside the doorway and brushed the dust off his trousers. It was dark, but he could see the front door ahead of him. It was closed. He walked to it, and pushed it with his hand. It didn't move. He gave it a harder push, and it swung open. The bottom of the door made a scraping sound as it pushed broken glass across the tiles on the floor. It was loud. He stood still, and waited.

'Hello?' he said. His voice cracked. He looked back at the boarded-up doorway, at the gap down at the bottom, and he waited. He turned back towards the front door. He cleared his throat and said in a louder, deeper voice, 'Boys, I saw the polis go by, you should get out of here, quick.'

When nobody came and nobody made a sound, he began walking through the front door. He walked slowly towards the bar, and looked around. He looked at the seats and tables, he looked at the floor and the walls. He stood still and looked everywhere. There were empty cans and bottles, empty packets of crisps, empty packets of fags. There was writing on the walls, and some of the seats had been slashed. There were pale patches on the walls behind the bar, where things used to hang or be screwed on, but had now been taken away. Towards the front of the pub, on the wall to the left, was a jukebox. The glass at the front of the jukebox had been smashed, and some of the cards that listed the albums had been pulled out and dropped on the floor. Some of them were on the tables, with small rectangles torn out of them.

Under the jukebox was a cushioned bench that ran along the left wall, then along the wall at the front of the pub, underneath where the window had been broken. He looked at the corner of the bench, where the bench on the left wall met the one at the front. He stood there looking at it for a long time. He walked over to it, then stopped. He looked over his shoulder to see if anybody was watching, but nobody was. He faced the bench, then leaned over to touch it. He touched the bottom, then he touched the backs. He stood upright, and smiled for a while, looking at the corner. Then the smile went away.

He turned to look behind him. On the right wall, opposite the bench on the left, were three booths. He looked at the middle booth. His top lip twitched. He blinked a single, slow blink.

He looked down at the bench beside him, at the corner, and sat down.

He closed his eyes for a while. When he opened them, he stood up and looked to the corner of the bench and began to speak.

'Gillian, what d'you want to drink?'

After he spoke, he looked around the pub to see if anybody was there, but nobody was. He looked back to the corner of the bench and said, 'One more then up the road?'

He walked towards the bar, smiling at the corner of the bench behind him. He stood on an empty bottle and stumbled. He stopped smiling and kicked the bottle away, smashing it against one of the high stools that were screwed into the floor at the bar.

He ran towards one of the stools and kicked it with the sole of his foot. He bounced back from it and landed on the floor. He got back on his feet and ran up to the stool again, kicking it harder, then again, until he heard something crunch. He walked over to the stool and began pulling it. He walked around the stool and stood between the stool and the bar, then crouched low to place his back against the cushion. He pushed his hands and feet against the bar to push his back against the stool. His teeth were clenched and his face was red with effort. The bolts at the bottom of the stool tore away from the floorboards. The man and the stool fell back against the floor.

He picked up the stool and walked over to the middle booth. He stepped backwards until he was as far back as he could go.

'Jamieson!' he shouted. 'Look!'

He ran towards the middle booth and threw the stool. It banged off the back cushion, leaving a hole in the fabric where somebody's head would be.

He sat on the floor.

A man appeared from a door behind the bar, wearing a suit and a hard hat. He saw that some drunk guy had broken into the pub, and was sitting on the floor.

'Here,' said the man. 'Here, you. You're not allowed in here. Get out. Go.'

'Go where, son?' said the drunk guy. 'Go where?'

The Speaker

Neil woke up to the sound of Tina's music. Her shite music.

He rubbed his eyes and turned to see if she was lying next to him, but he knew she wouldn't be. She was always up before him. Up for work.

She wasn't in the bedroom either. But the speaker was. The Bluetooth speaker, playing her music. The *portable* Bluetooth speaker, which she could easily have lifted and taken with her out the bedroom and into the kitchen or wherever else it was she was sitting. But she left it in the room on the set of drawers next to the bedroom window, which she'd got into the habit of doing these days, ever since Neil got into the habit of having his long lies in bed after his late nights on the computer.

But what did she expect him to do? There was no work, there were no jobs.

The song playing was something by John Lennon. Neil hated John Lennon. He wasn't that into The Beatles anyway, but he fucking hated John Lennon. Wife-beating cunt. But he wouldn't lie, that wasn't the main reason he hated him. It was something else, he didn't quite know. It was something to do with that effect they put on his voice. An echoey effect. It made him sound like he was singing in a tunnel. Or in a sewer. He sounded like he was singing in a fucking sewer. It was horrible. It was a horrible sound to wake up to.

Did Tina even like it? She used to say she liked John Lennon, years ago. That was back when they used to ask each other what music they were into, back when they first started going out. Back when they asked what music they were into and what films they liked and stuff they liked to take. She said she was into Radiohead and Muse and she mentioned John Lennon, and that was when he told her he hated John Lennon. That's how he knew that she knew.

It was no coincidence that it was John Lennon coming out that speaker.

He'd told her that he didn't like Radiohead either. He was alright with Muse somehow, even though he thought they sounded quite like Radiohead. And guess what she had playing not yesterday but the day before?

Radiohead.

She didn't play Muse, though.

He looked at the speaker. It was a good speaker. It cost a fair bit of money, and it was him that bought it. He bought it back when he could afford to splash out on a speaker that cost 150 quid. There were more expensive ones, bigger ones where you could plug your iPhone in at the top. This was a smaller one, but the sound was amazing. The bass.

He'd taken ages picking it. He'd made a cunt of buying the one they had before. It wasn't a speaker, it was a DAB radio, and Tina asked him why he bought it. He thought it would be good. It was a Sony, and all the reviews said the sound was good. But it was tinny as fuck. Tina said it wasn't like him to make a fuck-up like that. But the reviews said it was good.

They put up with it for a while, but it was shite. It wasn't just the sound that made it shite. It was the feeling it gave you, it was what it reminded you of, it reminded you that you'd bought something shite. It was the sound of putting up with something, that's what it sounded like. This tinny piece of shite.

He eventually asked himself why he didn't just use the money he earned and live it up a bit. Why not just buy something good? So he thought he'd buy a Bluetooth speaker. A good one. Bose. For the first time in ages, he'd splash out and buy something good.

150 quid was a lot for him, even when he was working. It was a lot just for a speaker.

And there it was now, playing John Lennon.

He looked at it, as it sat there on the drawers next to the window, and he could see that it had been moved from last night. It had been turned towards the bed. He was pretty sure it had been turned towards the bed again. It was hard to notice, but if you looked out for it, you could see it, you could see that it had been moved.

He first noticed it being moved a couple of weeks ago. The front of the speaker would normally sit in the middle of the drawers, at the front, facing forward. It wouldn't be turned slightly to the left or right, it would be facing forward. The front of the speaker was always parallel with the front of the drawers.

But recently, in the last couple of weeks, it had started to turn a bit towards the bed, so that the music blared in the direction of whoever was lying in the bed. Not towards the door, not towards the person who always stuck it on this early in the morning and then walked out the door, not towards the door. But towards the bed. And it wasn't him that turned it.

Every night, after Tina went to bed, he would stay up late, watching Netflix or a few films he'd downloaded. By the time he felt like going to sleep, he would go into the bedroom, and listen to hear if Tina was sleeping. And before getting into bed, he'd walk over to the drawers next to the window, and make sure the speaker was facing forwards. Directly forwards. He had to do that, because he wasn't sure if he was imagining it all.

The next morning, he would wake up and the speaker would be playing Tina's music, and when he looked, the speaker would be turned towards the bed. Tina herself wouldn't be in bed, she was never in bed when he woke up. She'd be walking around the house getting ready. And yet, the speaker would be pointed towards the bed.

It wouldn't be completely turned around, it wouldn't be at a 45-degree angle. It was subtle.

He didn't want to come right out and accuse her. He could be wrong. He'd been wrong about things like that before, like the time when the remote went missing and he said she was trying to fuck with his head, then he found it in his dressing-gown pocket. He didn't want to just come right out and accuse her, so he thought of theories that would let her off the hook, so that he didn't jump to conclusions.

He had a few theories that stopped him from coming right out and pointing the finger.

The first one was that she angled the speaker towards the bed so that she could hear it better herself when she was in bed in the morning. He was used to waking up and seeing her not there, but it could be the case that she liked lying in bed and listening to music for half an hour or so before he even woke up. She might get out of bed in the morning, turn the speaker towards her a bit, switch it on, then go back to bed, pick up the iPad and play her music. Then, when she got up, she just forgot to turn the speaker back to where it was facing. And forgot to switch it off, or take it with her into the kitchen or wherever she was.

But that one didn't stand up.

He reckoned that if she was getting up and turning the speaker towards the bed to listen to it, it would probably be turned towards the bed even more. There would be no reason to be subtle. Why turn it towards the bed by just one degree when you could turn it all the way around?

The second theory was that it was an accident. He thought that maybe when she switched it on in the morning, the force of her finger pressing down on the power button on the top of the speaker caused the speaker to slide, which caused it to turn. An innocent mistake, nothing more.

But that one didn't stand up either. He'd put it to the test last Thursday.

When the theory came into his head, he waited until she had left for work. Then he got up and tried it. He put the speaker back to its normal angle, facing directly forwards. Then he pressed the power button. But the speaker didn't budge an inch.

Even if he pressed the button at an angle, instead of directly down, the speaker didn't budge. It was to do with the rubber bits at the bottom of the speaker. The rubber stopped the speaker from sliding. It was possible, though, it was possible to push the speaker if you pushed towards the button at a really low angle, like maybe if she was crouched down. She could maybe be crouched down to open one of the drawers.

But!

The power button was on the left hand side of the speaker, and pushing towards it would cause the speaker to turn towards the left. But the bed was to the right. Pushing the button in that way would actually cause the speaker to turn *away* from the bed. And it most certainly wasn't turned away.

He had a third and final theory that came to him when he picked up the speaker to look at the rubber bits at the bottom. Maybe she picked the speaker up to switch it on, then she put it back down, and it just so happened to be angled towards the bed every time she put it back on the top of the drawers.

But that would have to be every time.

Every. Single. Time.

The exact same angle, the exact same subtle angle, every, single, time.

Forget it.

He really did hate John Lennon.

He remembered exactly where they were when he told her. They were in a bar on Gibson Street, a bar that isn't there anymore. It's still there as a bar, but it's different now. They were in there, and on came Radiohead. It was 'No Surprises' by Radiohead, and that got them talking about what music they were into.

They'd been shagging for a week, and had moved onto getting to know each other. Getting to know the wee things.

She started singing along to it. She just sang the chorus, during a break in their conversation. She sang it quietly while looking at him. But he pulled a face. He didn't mean to. Although he didn't like Radiohead, the face was mainly because he didn't really know what to do when somebody was singing and looking at you, it made him feel shy. So he did the face and she asked if he didn't like Radiohead, and he said no, not really. And that got them talking, about Radiohead. About Muse. And then he mentioned that he hated John Lennon.

That's how he knew that she knew.

She asked him what he did like, then. And he told her that he liked pop stuff. Eighties stuff. Stuff like eighties Kylie. She said that she liked eighties Kylie as well, and started singing the chorus to 'I Should Be So

Lucky'. He didn't sing along, he was too shy. He didn't want to show it, so he got talking instead, asking her if she liked other Kylie stuff from back then, like 'Turn It into Love' and 'It's No Secret'. But she wasn't really sure, she couldn't remember them or how they went. She asked him how they went, how 'Turn It into Love' went. He spoke the lyrics, but she said no, sing it, she wanted to know what the tune was like. He said no way, he knew she was trying to embarrass him, but she laughed and said she wasn't. Go, sing it. So he sang it. He got three or four words into the chorus, before she pointed and laughed at him singing. She was funny. He fucking knew she was going to do that, he knew she was at it.

And she was at it here.

With this speaker.

But it wasn't a funny thing. He'd take it as funny, if that's how it was intended, but it wasn't. That's not how she meant it.

The John Lennon song finished, and on came another one, by John Lennon. She was definitely at it.

He had an idea.

He leaned over and picked up the iPad from on top of her bedside cabinet. He went to her music app, tapped on Artists, tapped on K, scrolled through the songs, and tapped on the one he was after. The John Lennon song stopped.

He put down the tablet and quickly lay back in the bed, pulling the covers up to his nose. He'd pretend to be asleep.

It took a few seconds for his song to come on, and then on it came.

'Turn It into Love' by Kylie Minogue.

That Stock, Aitken and Waterman sound. People said at the time that it made all the songs sound the same, but that's what he liked. The bass line, the twinkling melody. It sounded brilliant on the speaker, it sounded better now than it did back then.

He waited for Tina to walk in.

Would she pop her head around the door and smile? Or would she march in and put Lennon back on? Something would happen one way or another. This is what it would take.

Kylie started singing, but there was still no reaction from Tina. No footsteps or creak of the door. He opened his eyes to see if she was standing there at the door. It would be good to see her dancing. It would be better to hear her singing.

He looked, but she wasn't there.

'Tina!' he shouted, but she didn't come.

He got out of bed and stuck on his boxers. He looked around the house, but she wasn't there.

He walked back to the bedroom and checked the time on the tablet. It was 10.14 a.m. She was long gone.

He'd get a job. He would. He'd love to get up in the morning and have somewhere to go and something to do.

What would be better would be to wake up and hear Kylie being played. To wake up and hear Kylie, knowing that it wasn't him that put her on.

But it had been a long time since Kylie had come out of that speaker.

Photography

Eric was out taking pictures with his new camera. He'd been looking for a hobby, looking for something to do, and this hobby was the latest.

He'd been looking around online, looking at things, and he'd come across some nice pictures that people had taken. Pictures of objects, or animals, or people, but they had a look to them that he could never get when taking pictures with his phone. They looked like something you'd see in a film. There would be a picture of a lamp post, but the stuff in the background behind the lamp post would be all blurry. He liked how that looked, and he wanted to know how it was done. He asked around online to find out what app it was, but people told him that it wasn't taken on a phone, it was taken with a camera. A camera-camera. A 'DSLR'.

He looked into it all, and it cost an arm and a leg. It wasn't just the camera that cost the money, but the lenses. In fact, some of the lenses, the big zoom ones, cost more than the cameras themselves. But he was just after the one that made the background blurry, and people told him to get a 50 mm lens. They called it the 'nifty fifty', and told him that it was ideal if he was after the blurry background effect, which he learned was called a 'shallow depth of field'.

He read up on what a shallow depth of field meant. There was so much to learn. But that's what he wanted, something to get into. Something to throw all his time and money into, something productive and positive to dive right into. Productive and positive.

He'd had the camera for a couple of weeks now, and he didn't really know what to take pictures of. He took pictures of the sorts of things he saw online, things that other people take pictures of. Pictures of street signs, or pictures of empty beer bottles. His pictures looked good. They looked all arty.

He took a picture of a dandelion, something he'd never really looked at since he was a boy. He'd walked past dandelions before and maybe had a glance, but he'd never seen them like this, with a shallow depth of field, with the dandelion crystal clear, but with everything else all blurry. It was a new way of looking at things. That's what photography was, he reckoned. It wasn't about saying, 'Look, here's how this thing looks.' It was about you having an idea of what something looks like, but if you looked closer, or saw it in a different light, or from a different angle, it would be different and new.

He would see something not that interesting, like a rusty lamp post. He'd take a picture of it. He'd focus on the lamp post, and then move the camera to the side a bit so the lamp post was to the right of the shot and the street was in the background to the left. He'd press the button to take a picture, then look at the screen to see how it turned out. There would be this one piece of rust on the lamp post, in focus, with the rest of the lamp post starting to go slightly blurry as it curved away from the camera. He thought about how it looked good on the camera, yet how it didn't look so good in reality. But if you thought about it, that *was* how it looked in reality, it just depended on how it was seen, either through the camera or through the eyes.

He took some more pictures of lamp posts, until they all began to look the same. He started to think of what else he could take pictures of.

There were people walking around, and he'd like to stop them and ask if he could take their picture, but he hadn't reached that stage yet. He wasn't at that level of photography yet, like some of the people he'd seen online. He wouldn't feel right doing that. He didn't even feel right being seen with the camera around his neck. People would see this guy taking pictures of the lamp posts and bottles and flowers, and they'd stare.

He thought it was best to get away from them. He looked down a street that led away from where the people were, away from the tenements and over towards the big business centre and the retail park. There weren't many people down that way, except for the ones in their motors. He began walking that way, until he was away from the passers-by.

He came to a stop at traffic lights, and took another picture. There were no people here, only wide roads and a motorway overhead. He pressed the button on the lights, and took a picture of the lit-up sign that said 'Wait'. He looked at the picture on the screen and it looked good. There was maybe some kind of meaning to seeing the word 'Wait'. Maybe not. He'd seen people online talking about certain pictures telling a story. There was a photo of a door handle that people had talked about, and they discussed the story it told. But maybe it was just a picture of a door handle.

He lifted his camera to take a picture of the red man across the road, but something else caught his attention, something to the left, something dark. He looked, and saw an underpass. It was an underpass that would take him under the street he was waiting to cross. It looked like it wasn't used often. It was manky, with holes in the wall and peeling paint. It looked like people used to go that way before the traffic lights were put up, and now it was easier to just press the button and wait.

The underpass took his interest. He lifted his camera to take a picture. He aimed it at the bottom of the stairs, where the underpass turned right to go under the street. He pressed the button then looked at the screen, expecting the picture to look as interesting as it was in his mind. But it wasn't. It looked like something he could have just taken on his phone.

He leaned to the side, next to the wall at the top of the stairs. He pointed the camera so that the wall at the side was out of focus, and the stairs leading down to the underpass were in focus, then he pressed the button. He looked at the screen, but it just looked like a picture of an underpass, except now it had a wall at the side. It just looked like how it looked.

He began to feel glum. He wanted this to work out. He breathed in through his nose and held his breath as he looked at the picture. He was aware that he was clenching his jaws, so he relaxed them and breathed out through his nose. He looked at the pole next to him, the one that held up the traffic lights, to see if there was any rust.

'Are you taking pictures?' came a guy's voice.

The guy was thin with cropped dark hair. He was wearing a thick Adidas jacket that looked too thick to be wearing here in June. His pupils were tiny, and there was some foam at the corner of his mouth.

Eric was about to answer, until a motorbike roared past on the road behind the guy. If Eric was the guy, the sound would have been enough to make him spin, but the guy turned slowly. He didn't react until a good two seconds after the bike had passed. 'Fuck was that?' said the guy to himself. He turned back towards Eric and smiled. Eric noticed that the guy's eyes didn't move in their sockets. 'You better not take my picture.'

The guy walked down the stairs towards the underpass. He reached the bottom and looked back at Eric, before turning right and walking through the tunnel under the road.

Eric took another deep breath and tried to relax his shoulders. He looked across the road at the red man, then looked down at the underpass again. He held up his camera to look at the screen, at the pictures he took before the guy had turned up. He looked at the last one he took of the underpass, the one with the wall to the side, and he deleted it. Then he deleted the one before.

He looked at the red man across the street, and lifted his camera to take a picture of it. He pressed the button, then had a look at the screen to see how it turned out, but he couldn't tell if it was good or bad. He didn't have an opinion. He lifted his camera to take another picture of the red man, but he didn't press the button. He lowered the camera and let it hang from his neck by the strap. He took a deep breath through his nose.

'Here,' said a voice. Eric looked towards it, towards the underpass, and breathed out. It was the guy again. He had reappeared at the bottom of the stairs. 'C'mere,' said the guy. 'There's something here. Look.'

Eric thought about it. He tried telling himself to not even consider it. He pushed the button on the traffic lights again.

'Look,' said the guy, pointing into the underpass. 'C'mon, I'm not going to hurt you.'

Eric walked down the stairs.

The guy smiled and waited for him. When Eric reached the last few steps, the guy walked into the underpass and said 'Over here', and Eric followed him in.

It was dark. There must have been lights in there before, but now they were either switched off or smashed, with the only light now being the daylight at either end of the tunnel. The guy pointed towards the middle of the tunnel, somewhere where there was nothing to see. 'It's just over here,' said the guy, as he walked that way. Eric followed behind.

He walked closer to the guy, then took his camera off from around his neck and wrapped the strap around the guy's throat. Eric expected more of a struggle, but the guy was lighter than he thought. The guy kicked Eric's shin with the back of his foot, but it didn't hurt. Eric swept the guy's feet from under him and swung him to the side. He pulled the strap tight with both his hands until his fists met at the back of the guy's neck. His arms began to shake.

Eric held him there for a minute. Then a minute more. Another bike roared past outside, but it sounded far away. He felt like he was underwater down here. It was because everything else felt far away, and it was cold and dark. And it was the way the guy was moving his hands about. He was barely moving, but his hands were moving slowly, reaching for the ground to try and support himself. It made him look like he was swimming.

Funny Face

Laura was with a lassie called Helen, who she hadn't seen for years. Over 20 years. Not since they were teenagers.

They'd arranged to meet up and have dinner in a restaurant, then the plan was to go somewhere afterwards to have some drinks, then maybe go to a club.

Laura was regretting it. She was regretting meeting up with Helen, because Helen was dull.

She wasn't the person that Laura remembered. Mind you, Helen was never that memorable to begin with. There was a crowd of them when she was younger, and Helen was a part of that crowd. But she was way in the background. Way, way in the background.

They'd bumped into each other last week. Laura had just left work and was heading for the train, when she heard somebody calling her name. 'Laura?' asked the voice. 'Laura McGilvray?'

When Laura looked, she saw a vaguely familiar face. A face from ages ago. The lassie pointed to herself. 'Helen,' she said. 'We used to hang about in Pollokshaws, remember?'

'Ah, that's right,' said Laura. 'Helen.'

Laura pretended that all these brilliant memories of Helen were coming back to her, when they weren't. All that Laura could remember was that Helen was one of the quiet ones, hardly saying anything at all. She was never much of a talker, she was never full of the patter, but Laura had a faint memory of how Helen would always get everybody laughing.

It was that face that she pulled. A funny face, with a funny voice.

Laura loved it. It wasn't an impersonation or anything pisstakey, it was just this funny face and this thing she used to say. They'd all get drunk, and then Laura would ask Helen to do that face she did, the face and the voice. She'd ask her to do it again and again. Helen would do it until she said that was enough. She was the type to leave you hungry, so that you never got fed up with it.

It was just a wee thing, just a funny face and voice, but it was so funny. That's why Laura had come out. A night out with somebody like Helen would be just what the doctor ordered.

But Helen wasn't funny. Not anymore.

'How was your meal?' asked Laura.

They'd finished eating a while ago, and Laura had already asked that question. She remembered she'd already asked, but she didn't care, because Helen wasn't saying much, and one of them had to say something.

'Yeah, nice,' said Helen.

Laura remembered that Helen had already said that as well.

Laura really regretted coming out tonight. She'd asked Helen lots of stuff about what she'd been up to since the old days, and Helen had answered with answers that were no longer than ten or twenty words. Laura would ask her about her family and where she stayed and what her job was, all the things like that, and Helen would answer. Then Helen would ask the same thing back. She'd never ask anything by herself, she'd never ask a question that she herself had come up with, it was always a question that Laura had asked first.

Another thing that Laura didn't like about being there was that Helen would look at her without speaking. When neither of them were speaking, she'd just look at Laura. It wasn't in a moody way or a flirty way, there was nothing behind it. But she'd just look at Laura, not saying anything, and Laura would have to fill in the silence with questions or by rabbiting away herself. A monologue. She didn't like talking about herself constantly, because that's normally something you criticise somebody for – she'd criticised people in the past for talking about themselves the whole night. But Laura had no choice. Helen was as dull as they came.

But she wasn't always.

Laura had to force herself to remember that. She reminded herself of why she said yes to meeting up. The face. The funny face. The face and the voice. It was so funny. Was that still there? Was that still there inside Helen? Laura looked at her and she couldn't imagine it. She couldn't imagine that dull, saggy face springing to life and making Laura laugh.

'Here,' said Laura, before gulping her wine. 'What was that face you used to do?'

'Face?' said Helen.

'Remember?' asked Laura. 'You used to do this face and put on a voice, I can't remember what it was.'

Helen frowned and looked off to think about it. She shook her head and said 'Nope'.

'Oh come on,' said Laura. 'You remember.' Then she remembered something herself. 'Wait, wait. Right, listen. Remember that time we were all in Callum's house?'

'Aye,' said Helen. 'When, though?'

'The time he had an empty,' said Laura. 'That time his maw and da were away on holiday and we all hung about there for the week. Remember that night somebody had a bottle of poppers?'

'I think so,' said Helen. 'I never liked poppers.'

'Right, but remember everybody was buzzing poppers, and then you'd do that face and the voice and everybody was howling?'

Helen thought about it again. She started to nod. 'Ah,' she said. 'I know what you're talking about now.'

'Thank God,' said Laura. 'I thought I was going mental there. You remember it?'

'Yeah,' said Helen. 'But that wasn't me.'

Laura, who was about to reach for the bottle of wine to pour herself another glass, stopped. 'What?' she asked.

'That's wasn't me,' said Helen. 'The face. That was Tracey.'

'Tracey?' asked Laura. She tried to remember who Tracey was, then it came to her. 'Tracey Elliott?'

'Yeah.'

Laura thought back to Tracey Elliott. It was hard. Long time ago. And Laura had had a drink. She couldn't picture the funny face on Tracey right away, so first she thought of Tracey's normal face. When it came to her, she then saw Tracey pulling the funny face and doing the voice.

And there it was.

It was Tracey. It was Tracey Elliott she'd been thinking about.

'Oh,' said Laura. 'I thought it was you.'

'No,' said Helen.

Laura smiled at her, waiting for her to say something. She waited for Helen to perhaps say something about the mix-up and the face. Perhaps she would say how it was funny that Laura thought it was Helen that did the face, because Helen and Tracey didn't look the same. They were both kind of quiet, but they weren't two people you'd normally get mixed up.

Laura was going to talk about the mix-up, but instead she waited for Helen to do it. But Helen didn't. Instead, Helen just had a sip of her drink and looked out the window. Then she looked back at Laura, without saying anything. That thing again of just sitting there looking without saying anything. Back to that.

Laura thought about the funny face again. If Helen wouldn't talk about it, Laura would. There was nothing else to talk about.

'It was funny that,' said Laura. 'That face. Plus the voice she did as well.'

'Yeah,' said Helen.

'What was it again?' asked Laura. 'Can you remember?'

'What was what?'

'The face. What was it she did again? What was it she said?'

'I can't remember,' said Helen.

'But …' said Laura.

She was ready to ask how Helen could remember that it was Tracey who used to do the funny face yet not be able to remember what the face was, or what was said. But it was fair enough. It was like trying to remember the faces that Phil Cool used to do, him that was on the telly when they were younger. All he did was funny faces, but if you tried to remember or actually pull the faces he did, you probably couldn't do it. So it was fair enough.

Laura was going to drop it. But then she remembered that she'd just said 'But …' and Helen hadn't then asked her 'But what?'

Normally if somebody said 'But' and then didn't finish, you'd be wanting to know what they were going to say, but Helen wasn't. She just sipped her drink and looked out the window, and then looked at Laura.

Back to looking at Laura again without saying anything.

They had arranged to go somewhere for drinks and then head to a club. This would be how it was for the rest of the night. Laura had thought it was Helen who did the funny face, but it wasn't.

'Can you not remember?' asked Laura.

'Remember what?' asked Helen.

'The face, the face. The face, or the voice. Or what she said?'

'I don't know,' said Helen. 'I can't remember'

'See if you can do it,' said Laura, sitting back in her seat. 'Let's see if we can remember.' She clapped her hands and rubbed them together.

Helen humoured Laura with a smile, then looked out the window.

'Helen,' said Laura.

Helen turned back to look at her.

'Let's see if we can remember,' said Laura. 'See if you can do it. Go.'

Helen smiled and shook her head, then sipped her drink.

'Oh, come on,' said Laura. 'Go, give it a try. C'mon, do it.'

Helen looked out the window. This time, she didn't even reply with either a word or a smile. This person who had invited Laura out to catch up, who had sat there for over an hour without barely speaking a word unless spoken to, just looked out the window.

'Helen,' said Laura, making Helen look at her again.

'What?' asked Helen.

'Do it.'

Helen smiled again and spoke quietly, like she was

speaking to a child. 'Nooooo,' she said, and went to pick up her drink again.

'Then do *something*,' said Laura. 'For fuck sake, do *something*.'

The Bike

Tony was talking to his wife Barbara. She was still in bed, but he'd got up early and was putting on his jacket in front of her.

He told her that he'd make her a nice breakfast, a nice Sunday morning breakfast. Bacon, eggs, black pudding, baked beans, anything she wanted. She normally made it, but this time he felt like doing it himself. A treat.

'We don't have any bacon,' she said. 'Plus we're out of butter.'

'Do we not?' he asked. 'I knew we never had any black pudding, but I thought we had the rest.' Then he shrugged and said, 'Ah well, I was going over to the shops anyway. For the black pudding.'

Barbara said, 'Well, if you go and get that, I'll make it.' And she began to sit up.

'No, no,' said Tony, putting his hands up. 'I'll make it. I'll make it.' Then he said, all proud of himself, 'Breakfast in bed.'

She wasn't sure. She was grateful of the gesture, but he'd made fry-ups before and they weren't good. The toast would be cold, the eggs would be too runny or overdone. You name it. It was nice of him to offer, but he wasn't very good. She remembered the one he made her earlier that month, and she'd prefer it if he'd just brought her a bowl of cereal.

But she smiled and said, 'All right. Thank you very much.' And she lay back in bed again. Tony zipped up his coat and left.

He walked out the house, and repeated to himself the things he had to get. 'Eggs, bacon. Beans, baked beans. Black pudding. Bacon.' No, he'd already said bacon.

There was something else, but he'd remember it when he got there.

He walked down his street and onto the main road, and then along to the traffic lights.

'Butter,' he said to himself. He was to get butter. 'Butter, eggs, bacon, baked beans, black pudding …'

He wasn't sure if there was anything else. Then he reckoned that the best way to remember was simply to imagine having a fry-up, and imagine what was on the plate.

THE BIKE

He crossed the road without walking to the traffic lights – there weren't many motors on the road this early. There weren't many people walking about either. There was a cyclist locking up his bike to a lamp post; there was a young woman in her gym gear, walking her dog; there was a teenager with a hooded top, going into the garage. People up early to keep fit, or sent out to get breakfast. It was a nice morning for it, he was glad he came out.

He took a deep breath of the fresh air, and headed for the garage. He was to get butter, bacon, black pudding … och, he'd work it out when he walked in there.

He stopped for a second to watch the cyclist. The guy was having trouble with his bike. With his lock. He was mumbling to himself. Swearing. Then he turned to see Tony looking at him.

Tony smiled, and was about to say something to him, but the guy just looked back to his bike lock. Not a happy camper.

'Morning,' said Tony. 'You know, you don't …'

'What?' said the cyclist.

The cyclist was in a cunt of a mood. He looked at Tony, then looked back at his lock. He held it in his hand, unlocked, then he looked at the bike, as if trying to work out how to solve the problem in his mind before doing it for real.

Tony didn't want to annoy the guy. He knew how it was with these folk. Cyclists. Especially ones like this, the ones that wore all the gear like they were in that Tour de France. Highly strung. He'd seen a few of them get angry at drivers over next to nothing. Shouting at the top of their lungs.

He was sure it went both ways, though, he wasn't judging the guy. Tony reckoned that both sides just needed to turn it down a notch. Not just the folk on the bikes, but the folk on both sides. Turn the other cheek, as the saying goes. Just look at this glorious day – how can you be off to a bad start on a fresh day like this? A fresh, bright morning.

'Fuck sake,' mumbled the guy, but it wasn't at Tony. He was crouched, trying again to get his lock around his bike and the lamp post, but he couldn't quite do it. There was a sign for a cafe in the way. The sign was strapped to the bottom of the lamp post. The cyclist was able to slide the sign up the pole only so far, but not far enough.

Tony said, 'All I was going to say was that you don't need to lock your bike up here, son.' And Tony truly believed that. It was a good area. He'd lived here for over 30 years without any sense of it being a bad area or getting worse over time. Even the teenagers, you didn't get any hassle from them, not back then and not now. They were good boys. It was a good area.

The cyclist didn't move. He was holding his lock, but he wasn't doing anything.

Tony didn't know what to say. He didn't know what the guy was doing. He almost looked like he was about to cry. Tony had felt that way himself before, trying to put up a shelf or what have you. You feel like you're having a fucking breakdown.

'What I mean is,' said Tony, but the cyclist had something else to say.

He stood away from the bike, looked at Tony, and said, 'Go'.

Tony looked at him and said, 'What?'

'Go,' said the guy. 'On you go.'

On you go what? 'I don't know … I don't know what you …'

Then the guy said something under his breath. Tony could hear that the guy was 'sick to fucking death of' something.

The teenage boy with the hooded top left the garage, and walked past them both. The cyclist watched him, then looked to Tony and smiled.

'Is it him, aye?' said the cyclist.

The teenager looked at the cyclist, not sure if he was being spoken to. He kept walking. Tony didn't know what was going on here - who was the cyclist talking to? What was the mix-up here?

The cyclist spoke to the teenager. 'D'you think

I'm fucking daft?' he said. 'Go then,' pointing to his bike.

The teenager kept walking. He reached into his pocket for his phone, but kept on walking.

'Go then,' said the cyclist to Tony, and then he grabbed Tony's arm. It hurt.

'What you doing, son? What is this?'

'D'you want a wee shot, aye?' asked the guy. 'Is that it? A wee shot around the block, is that all? Go then. On you go. D'you think I'm fucking daft?'

Tony pulled his arm away.

The cyclist lightened up. 'On you go,' he said, smiling. 'Have a go.' He was suddenly cheerful.

'I don't want a go,' said Tony. 'Son, what is this?'

'On you go,' said the cyclist. 'It's just a bike. A wee cycle around the block, aye? D'you want a wee cycle around the block, aye, is that it? And you'll bring it right back?'

This was all going too fast for Tony. The guy with the bike seemed nice enough, but there was something not right with him; one minute he looked ready to go for Tony's throat, the next he was full of the joys of spring.

Was it the teenager? What was the thing with the teenager? Did the teenager try to steal his bike before or something? Tony didn't know. He didn't think so. It was a good area, this. He might even know the boy.

'On you go,' said the cyclist, pointing to the handle-bars. 'There's the brakes, these are the gears. It's a good bike, you'll love it. Carbon frame. Cost £1,995. And it's all yours, if you promise to bring it back. Do you promise?'

This was a wild morning.

But, you know, maybe he would. Maybe Tony would have a shot. He'd have something to tell Barbara when he got back. And he'd be able to show this guy that this wasn't a bad area. Tony meant what he said, he didn't have to lock his bike up here. He didn't know about that teenager, he couldn't vouch for him person-ally, but he knew that most of them were fine. No hassle at all.

'All right then,' said Tony, and he took the bike.

'That's it,' said the guy. He was speaking to Tony like he was a child. 'Up you get, that's it.'

Tony sat on the bike, and put his hands on the handlebars.

'Oh, it's been a while,' said Tony.

'That's right,' said the guy. 'Who is it, by the way? Was it him?'

'Was who what?' asked Tony.

The guy pointed back the way, in the direction the teenager had gone.

'I don't know about him,' said Tony. 'But I know that this is a good area, son. I'll show you.'

'You do that,' said the guy. 'Who cares, eh? It's only a bike.'

The guy held onto the seat of the bike and began pushing. Tony wobbled the front wheel from left to right.

'I've never been on something like this,' he said. 'Here, wait. Wait.'

The guy pushed Tony faster and faster until he couldn't keep up. Tony liked it, but he reckoned that was enough.

He looked over his shoulder at the guy, and smiled. The guy was becoming further and further away, but Tony could see the guy smile back. Then the guy looked down at the pavement.

Tony looked forward to see where he was going. He didn't want to go over a broken bottle and cause the guy any trouble.

He looked back over his shoulder. He wanted to tell the guy that he wanted to come off now. He could see that the guy was still looking at the pavement. The guy wasn't smiling anymore. He was hitting the sign on the lamp post with his bike lock.

Then, all of a sudden, the guy started sprinting after Tony.

There was a look on the guy's face that Tony didn't like. It looked like maybe the guy was just concerned about Tony's safety and the safety of his bike, but as the guy got closer, it looked less like that and more like something else.

It made Tony want to pedal faster. And so he did. He pedalled until the guy became further and further away. He pedalled until all he could hear was the wind in his ears.

He didn't get back until two that afternoon.

Barbara knew he'd ruin breakfast. And he did.

Bericht

Benidorm

Me and the lads fucked off to Benidorm there. Fucked off for the weekend. A wee Friday to Sunday thing. We do it every year, pretty much. I jump online and get us a wee deal and then we're off. It was some fucking laugh.

This year it was me, Peter, Scott and Scott's uncle Andy. Just the four of us. There used to be a lot more, more than a dozen, but they've all dropped out. Every year it's like one less is up for it. Even though we always have a laugh, by the time I start talking about where we can go next time around, everybody's like that: 'I'm not really up for it.'

I'd be like: 'You're not really up for what? Having a laugh?'

And they'd be like: 'I'm up for having a laugh, I just don't fancy Benidorm,' or Magaluf, or wherever else

I suggested. And if I told them to suggest somewhere else, they'd be like: 'Och, I'm just a bit skint right now.'

It was bullshit.

The fact was that they wurnae up for it anymore. Getting old. The cunts couldnae handle it anymore, that was the sad fact of reality. So it was just the four of us this time. We were down to four.

Funny thing is, we ended up being down to three, cos of what happened at the airport. I've got this wee game, right? It's a wee game I made up for whenever we're in the airport. It's called Bomb.

So we're there at the airport, Glasgow Airport, and we're waiting in the queue at the security bit. A big fucking queue winding back and forward like a snake, the thing barely moving. We were right in the middle of it, about halfway to go. Another 20 minutes at least.

I don't mind queuing, cos time flies when you're having fun. But we wurnae. We wurnae having fun. And it was because of Scott. Well, Scott's maw. She was in hospital, so everybody was being pure sombre. No cunt saying anything, no patter. Scott was especially gutted, not just because it was his maw, but because it was Scott that put her there.

What happened was, he was at her house, helping her move some furniture. He was moving this couch, and he somehow managed to break her foot with it. So she had to get taken in for an operation. The operation went fine, but Scott told me that she'd have to use a wheelchair for a couple of months. His family fell out with him, nobody was talking to him, and he felt pure terrible. But other than that, everything was fine. A broken foot, no big deal.

Then guess what.

She got one of they fucking hospital bugs.

You know that sort of shite you hear about in the news, a supervirus or superbug or whatever it is? It actually happened to Scott's maw. So then suddenly it's went from a broken foot to her being on the brink of death.

When Scott told me, I was like that: 'Here, imagine she died and there's you at the funeral. The minister's like that: "We are gathered here today to say goodbye to Janet McDonald. Killed by a couch."'

He couldnae laugh, though, that's how bad he felt. Pure guilty as fuck. Then he told me that he wisnae coming to Benidorm. His maw was getting better, but he wanted to stay at the hospital until she had a full recovery. A few days later, though, he phones back saying that his family just told him to go on his holiday and they'd let him know when she got out. I was like that: 'They're right, Scott. You've done more than enough.'

So there we were in the queue at the airport.

Scott's staring into space, thinking about his maw, and Andy and Peter are in that sombre way. Now, I don't know about you, but if I'm in a downer the best medicine is having a laugh. That's what everybody says, in't it? You have to agree with that.

So I was like that to myself: Fuck this, let's get a game of Bomb on the go.

With Bomb, what you've got to do is: the first person says 'Bomb', all quiet, as quiet as they can. Then the next person's got to say it louder. Then the person after that, then the person after that, until something happens. It's a fucking buzz, honestly. I remember it being a buzz even before 9/11.

Before 9/11, you'd get to say 'bomb' about 20 times before any of the staff took notice. You'd see some cunt in a suit walking about, trying to find out who was making the racket, then you'd stop. You'd be shiting it that they'd find out it was you, but all they would have done in they days was give you a stiff talking to. We never got caught, but if we did, we'd probably have just got told to keep the noise down.

These days it's a different story. Especially there in Glasgow Airport. Mind they cunts that tried to blow the place up a few years back? Aye, it's a different story now. But honestly, it's some fucking buzz. Try it.

So I was like that: right, let's get a game of Bomb on the go.

I gave everybody a wee tap on the arm to get their attention. Even Scott. And I went like this, pure quiet: 'Bomb.'

Andy was like that: 'What?', cos he's never played it before. Andy hisnae come with us on holiday that much. I don't always invite him. He must be about 60 or something, he's a wee alky. He was only there to make up the numbers. He said it would be good to come along cos then he could give Scott support. That's what he said: 'support'. But he couldnae support fuck all. He's a daft wee alky.

So Andy didnae know what I was on about. The rest of them knew, though, but they wurnae up for it. Scott was in his trance, thinking about his maw. Peter smiled. I got a wee smile from Peter. He looked away and went 'Nawwww', but he had a wee smile on his face like he could be persuaded. Like he was playing hard to get. I like Peter.

He's an accountant, right? Peter. And I bet that sounds like he's a right fucking bore. I bet that all these folk he deals with, all these clients and that, think he's the most straight-laced cunt in the world. But he's always been up for a laugh, right back to when we were wee. You just go like that: 'C'mon and we'll do this,' and it disnae matter how mental it is, if you ask him enough, he'll do it.

Andy was like that to me again: 'Kenny, son, what did you say?', leaning in, speaking all quiet like I'm bitching about somebody. His breath humming of booze. A wee alky. He'd probably been drinking since the crack of dawn.

So I explained the rules to him, and he chuckles and goes: 'Naw, you're alright.'

And that was the end of that. I wisnae gonnae just play it with Scott, you cannae just play it with two, cos that would mean there's a 50/50 chance that you'll be the one that gets caught. And fuck that. I like a buzz, but fuck that.

But then I hear this voice, this voice that wisnae from any of us.

'Imbecile.'

I looked behind me and there was this old guy standing ahead of me in the queue. Some old guy with white hair and a beetroot face. He looked like he was just back from holiday, all sunburnt, but he wisnae. His face was just red, with high blood pressure or something. One of these short-fuse types. Easy as fuck to wind up.

I said to Andy: 'Ooof, Andy, you taking that?'

Andy was like that to him: 'What? What's that, fella?' Andy was clueless.

The old guy turned around and said: 'No, not you. I meant your friend there,' pointing at me. 'The police here, they won't mess around. I'm just giving you a friendly warning.'

I was like that: 'You hear that, Andy? He's warning you.'

Andy was like that to him: 'Here, fella, I'm warning *you*!'

Clueless.

I went like that to Andy: 'Fuck him, mate. Right, c'mon.' Then I whispered 'Bomb', and pointed to Andy to tell him it was his turn to go.

Andy went for it. He went: 'Bomb.' He said it a bit louder than me, then looked at the old guy.

The old cunt shook his head and turned away, and Andy looked all pleased with that.

I nodded at Peter to go, but he said, 'Naw, Kenny. No way,' then he took a wee step away from us, like a bomb really was about to go off. I let him away with it, though, because we only needed three people. I'm all right with a one in three chance of getting caught, and I knew we'd have that as long as I got Scott to join in as well.

I looked at Scott, but it was like he hidnae heard a word. He was tuned out. The thing with his maw had really hit him bad. I gave him a nudge and went, 'Go, Scott, your turn. C'mon, it'll be a laugh,' but Scott didn't do anything. He didnae even look at us.

Andy started getting cold feet, seeing the state of Scott. Scott's his nephew, remember, and he went like that to me: 'C'mon, Kenny, leave him. His maw, you know?'

But I was only trying to have a laugh. I thought it might have even helped Scott a bit, who knows. It's better than all this sombre shite hanging over him like a raincloud.

I went like that to Scott again: 'Go!', and gave him another nudge. 'Say "bomb".'

Scott went like that: 'Bomb.'

It was quiet as fuck, though. He still wisnae looking at any of us. He looked like some cunt full of pills in a mental hospital. So I went like that: 'No chance, Scott. Louder than that, ya cheating bastard.'

And he went: 'BOMB!' It was loud as fuck. Loud enough for everybody in our bit in the queue to go quiet. Then he went like that again: 'BOMB!', still staring at the ground.

I was like that: 'Alright, Scott. Fucking hell, mate. Fuck!' I looked around to see what the consequences were gonnae be, and there was the polis walking over, following the direction of where all the heads were turned.

Peter went like that: 'Oh, yous are fucked now.'

I went like that: 'No, *you're* fucked,' not even knowing what I meant. I was fucking buzzing.

I looked at Scott. He hidnae taken his eyes off the ground. The cunt was a million miles away. I said to Peter: 'Look at the state of Scott, man, you cannae let Scott take the hit. Look at him!'

Peter was like that: 'It's not my fault.'

I said: 'It is your fault. It was your fucking turn.' I looked to Andy and went, 'It was his fucking turn, win't it?', pure trying to get him onside.

Andy went like that: 'Aye.'

Peter was looking at us like we were mental, the smile wiped right off his face. He was like that: 'What the fuck yous on about?'

I went: 'That was your turn, Peter. Scott widnae have shouted that if it was your turn, would he?'

Peter was like that: 'You're talking fucking shite,' and I was, but the polis were getting closer and I could see the panic getting to him. And remember with Peter that if you just keep at it, he'll buckle.

I said: 'Peter, just tell them it was a joke, tell them it was you, tell them it was a joke and they'll be alright with it.'

Peter was like that: 'Fuck off, Kenny. I didnae say it, I was the only cunt that didnae.'

Then Andy chips in with: 'But it was your turn!'

Daft Andy chipping in, that was funny. Cos I bet you any money he didnae really know what was going on. If I had went like that to him: 'What d'you mean, Andy? How was it Peter's turn?' he widnae have known.

But I said: 'He's right, Peter. Andy's right.'

I could hear a woman say 'Over there, officer'. And that made me shite it.

I went up close to Peter and said: 'Look. Scott's maw's in hospital, Peter. All right? Just tell them you were joking, talk your way out of it. For fuck's sake, man, do the right thing!'

I was trying to look pure considerate, but inside I was nearly hitting the giggles.

Peter looked at me, then he looked at Scott and Andy. Then this voice comes from the side of the queue, pure deep: 'Okay, can I ask who caused the disturbance just then? Can you step out, please?'

It was the polis. It wisnae the kind of polis that carries a gun, but still. And next to him was this other guy with a name badge thing hanging from his neck, with this look on his face, this pure serious look to let us know that the situation was severe.

I looked at Peter. Then Peter went like that to the polis: 'It was just a joke.'

The cunt got dragged from the queue. And that was that. We all looked away like we barely knew him.

He's a fucking goner, man. I'm telling you. That company he works in, that accountant place, it's one of they big places, the type with all these surnames joined together. Bigshots. They willnae be putting up with that behaviour, no way. Funny as fuck, though. I like Peter and everything, but it was funny as fuck.

So we gets to the hotel.

We gets there about 4, 5 o'clock. Nice hotel. 3 stars, I think it was, cheap as fuck, and a lot nicer than I thought it would be. You could see the pool from the reception. Big fucking pool. About 20 people were standing around the edge of it, all doing this dance to some song, with some guy on a mic telling them what to do. It was a kind of Macarena thing, except the song was one of they old ones about doing the twist. It looked good.

I was like that to Scott and Andy: 'Look at this, eh?' Cos it was a surprise to me, how good the place was. I didnae look at the place when I booked it, I never really do. All I'm interested in is that it isnae too far from the action, that it's cheap, and that we can all get a room together. That's important, that. Getting a room together.

It's not cos we're all shagging each other or anything, it's because it's more of a laugh that way. I remember we all used to get separate rooms. Everybody split into about ten different rooms. I didnae like it. Like if we were out at a pub and I'm pure ripping the piss out of one of them, they could just fuck off to their room in a huff, and there was nothing you could do about it. So I started booking rooms where we could cram about six or seven of us in at a time. No escape. If you fuck off in a huff, we'll turn up later when you're sleeping and fart on your head.

It was a room for four this time. Except, obviously, it was just for three, cos of what happened to Peter. When we checked in at the reception, the receptionist lassie went: 'And, uh, where is, uh, Peter, uh, how do you say this? McKinnon?'

I just went like that: 'Guantanamo.'

It was a wee joke, because Peter was probably getting questioned by the counter-terrorism lot. I looked at Scott and Andy, thinking I'd get a wee smile, but I got nothing. I know, it's shite for Peter and everything, but it's funny. It is funny. But not so much as a smile from Andy. And Scott wisnae even listening. He was still in his trance, holding his phone. And I was thinking: is this my holiday? Is this what the whole holiday's gonnae be like?

These birds went walking by.

So I went like that to Scott: 'Scott, mate. Scott,' and I nodded my head to them. I looked at Scott to see what he thought. I wanted to inject a bit of life back into him, via his cock. Get the blood pumping, get some energy about him. He looked at them for a second or two, with no expression, then he just went back to looking at his phone.

I was thinking: that isnae good. That isnae a good sign. It's Scott that I go pulling with. It's always best when you've got somebody else with you, a bit of company, a bit of a crowd. But it was looking like I was on my tod, cos I wisnae exactly gonnae go pulling with Andy. He's about 60, remember. A daft wee alky.

But here's what happens.

There were three of them, three of these lassies. They were wearing shorts and flip-flops and they were carrying their bags, cos that was them finished sunbathing for the day, but they still had on their bikini tops. So you'd think I'd be looking at their tits. But naw. I was looking at this lassie's belly.

It wisnae because she had a pure flat belly or anything. It was because she didnae. Her mates had flat bellies, they were all slim, like they go to the gym a lot. But this one, she was short and a wee bit fat. She looked like she didnae give a fuck.

Her shorts were tight, making her midriff stick out, that whole muffin top thing, and she had a piercing in her belly button. You'd get lassies that would try to hide a belly like that, guys as well, but there's her with it on show, with this wee sparkly thing in it like a belly dancer. That's like the opposite of hiding it. She didnae give a fuck.

I looked back to her face, and I saw that she'd seen me.

Caught.

I said to her: 'Excuse me, where is there to go here?'

That's a wee thing I do if I do get caught looking. I just start talking, about anything. I just pretend that I was looking at her cos I wanted to ask her something.

She went: 'Sorry?'

She was English. And she smiled. I wisnae sure if she had seen me looking at her belly after all, or if she just didnae care. I went: 'We've just got here, where is there to go tonight, d'yous know?'

And one of her pals went like that right away: 'TT. Typically Tropical. Cheap drinks but the staff are shit.'

And the lassie with the belly was like that to them, 'Fuck off,' and gave them the finger, still smiling. She told us that she worked there, that's what that bit of patter with her mate was all about.

I looked at Scott to see if he was taking an interest in all this, but no. Looking at his fucking phone. It looked pure ignorant.

I looked back at the lassie and went like that: 'Where? Tropical?' cos I only made out the word 'Tropical'.

She went like that: 'Yeah.'

But I meant that I only heard the word 'Tropical', and I was wanting her to fill in the blanks. I was gonnae ask again, but I didnae want to push it, I didnae want to come across as too keen. I liked her and everything, but I didnae know if she liked me, I didnae want to freak her out. So I went like that: 'Awright, we might head round on Sunday, see how it goes,' like I could take it or leave it.

She said: 'All right. But it's the karaoke party tonight, you don't wanna miss that!' Then her and her mates left the hotel.

I looked out the window to watch them, and heard the one with the belly say something like 'Yeah, I love that accent', and then 'Scottish accent' or 'Sexy accent'.

Ooooof. What a start to the holiday.

I looked at Scott and said: 'We are going there. We are fucking going there *tonight*!' But the cunt was looking at his phone. I went like that: 'What did she say, Scott? Something Tropical. Scott, mate. Scott,' snapping my fingers. Scott kind of tilts his head up like he's about to look at me, but he didnae take his eyes off his phone. So I was like that to Andy: 'Andy, what did she say the name of that place was?'

Andy was like that, steaming: 'I don't know. Tropical, I think. Tropical.' Alky cunt. They gave him one drink on the flight but they widnae let him have any more, that's the state he was in. They could tell he was out of it, even with him sitting down.

The receptionist finished doing her stuff on the computer and gave us our keycards and told us where to go. I looked at Scott and Andy while the receptionist lassie was telling us it all, and they wurnae listening to that either. They just wurnae interested in the holiday one bit. We headed to the lift and I pushed the button for our floor and up we went. About halfway up, the lift stops and the door opens at one of the floors, but nobody was there. I got out, just to see what Scott and Andy would do. And guess what? They followed me out. So I jumped back in the lift as the door was shutting. And they didnae find the room for about half an hour. Haha, useless pair of cunts.

When they turned up, we all got ready. I sprayed on some aftershave and we headed out. I was obsessed with finding that bird. Obsessed.

I looked on my phone, searching for 'Tropical' and 'Benidorm', thinking it would be a doddle, but it turned out that there were about five places in Benidorm with the word 'Tropical' in them, dotted all about the place, and none of them rang a bell. It was gonnae be an adventure, but I was up for it. It was a cracking night for it. It was a mild night. A T-shirt night. We walked down the beachfront, this big street with all these restaurants and cafes facing the sea, playing music, with people inside having their dinner and having drinks, watching the sun setting. There were people still on the beach, lying on towels, even though the sun was going down. It was that kind of weather, that kind of night. Warm and busy. There were groups of lads having a laugh, laughing loud. There were families. Old folk. Everybody smiling and laughing. Groups of lassies walking by, all tarted up, hitting you with this big waft of perfume.

And there were these cunts. These cunts I was with.

Scott was still staring at his phone. The cunt had barely said a word since we touched down. As for Andy, Jesus fucking Christ. We'd get to one of these pubs with 'Tropical' in the name, and I'd ask the staff if they had a karaoke night on, and they widnae know what I was on about, so I just wanted to keep moving to find the next one. I just wanted to find this lassie. But Andy was like that: 'C'mon and we'll just stay here.' Every time. I'd be telling him naw, cos this wisnae the pub we were looking for. Then it would be another half-hour trek to the next Tropical. Have they got a karaoke party? Naw. And there would be Andy asking if we could just stay and have a drink there anyway. Another half-hour trek. Karaoke party? Naw. Andy asking if we could have one in there. Every fucking time.

I sound like a grumpy as fuck cunt, but I'm not, honestly. I'm the furthest from a grumpy cunt you can get. But see if you compared it to how things used to be, when there used to be about fucking 15 of us walking down the street, having a laugh, pulling birds, see if you compared that to this? You'd get it. You'd get it then. You'd be giving me a pat on the back. You'd be giving me a cuddle.

We got to the second or third last one of these Tropical pubs on the map. Nae karaoke. I was like: 'Let's go. Next.'

Andy was like: 'How can we not just stay here?'

I said: 'Cos some of us are wanting our hole, Andy. Some of us can still get it up.' I grabbed his cock and gave it a shoogle. I was laughing, but I was raging.

He stepped away and went: 'Och, I don't think Scott's got that on his mind right now, you know?'

He was right. There was Scott looking at his phone, his face tripping him. So I snatched it off him.

Scott was like: 'Gie's it, Kenny. Gie's my phone back.'

Andy was like that: 'C'mon, Kenny, give him his phone. He needs it for his maw.'

I was like: 'Naw. Naw, Scott. Naw. I'm keeping the phone. You're here to have a laugh. I'm keeping it. You're maw's fine, mate.'

He was like: 'Naw, they've not been texting. They were texting this morning but now no cunt's telling me anything, something's up.'

I said: 'Mate, they're probably sick to fuck of you texting, that's all. Remember it was you that did it, it was you that stuck her there.'

Andy was like that: 'Oh come on now, below the belt.'

But it was fucking true, and Scott knew it. It shut him right fucking up.

I stuck his phone on silent, shoved it in my pocket and pointed at the pub they all wanted to go in. I went, 'Right, there's your stupid fucking pub. Let's go then.'

And in we went to this shitey, miserable wee bar full of couples and old folk watching *Only Fools and Horses* on this projector screen.

We all sat there getting steaming, getting drinks brought to us. Pints, sangria, ouzo, the lot. I would have been all right with it, if I didnae know that that lassie was waiting for me elsewhere. Dancing, maybe. Laughing.

Scott kept asking me if anybody had texted or phoned. Asked me about a hundred times. Every time there was a wee quiet bit in *Only Fools and Horses*, I'd see him out the corner of my eye, looking over to me. He'd lean over and go: 'Sorry to ask, Kenny, but anything yet?', and every time he did, I'd say 'Naw'. He was doing my nut in. But then I started having a laugh with it.

He'd ask me if there had been any texts, so I'd pull his phone out my pocket and have a look at it, then pretend to be pure devastated at what I was reading on the screen. Then I'd say 'Naw'.

At one point when he asked me, I looked at the phone and said: 'Scott, mate, can I speak to you for a second? I'm not joking this time.' I got up and led him away from the pub, right round the corner away from the noise. And I went like that: 'Naw.'

I was fucking howling. He stopped asking after that.

So we sat there watching *Only Fools and Horses*. I don't know what time we stayed till, but we were legless by the end of it. We'd definitely stayed long enough to watch the episode with the chandelier twice and the long one with the watch where they become millionaires. Plus *Fawlty Towers*, the one where he does the funny walk.

Nobody had texted or phoned. Nothing. But when we got to the room that night, I checked the phone and there were two or three missed calls, and a text from somebody saying that they tried to phone and that Scott was to phone back. I remember reading it and thinking: I hope she's fucking dead, man. I just thought: 'See if she's dead? Good.' I know that's snide, but I was pure giggling under the covers. I fucking needed it.

I woke up the next morning with a cunt of a hang-over, a cunt of a headache and a hard-on.

I'd have fucking loved to have woke up next to that lassie, in her hotel room or wherever, with her pulling my knob. I'd love to have woken up with her and talked for a bit, the pair of us slagging a few things off, taking the piss out each other. It could have happened anaw. If I'd found her the night before, we would have definitely been shagging, I'd have been waking up with her, the pair of us smiling, and this would have been a different story. But I knew that wisnae gonnae happen, even before I opened my eyes. The room was stinking of farts and feet, and I could hear Andy snoring.

I opened my eyes and looked about the room to see if Scott was up. It was a nice room, by the way, a nice big room with everything in it, everything in the one room. A wee kitchen, a couple of single beds, and a fold-out bed couch thing. I was on one of the single beds, there was Andy snoring on the other, sleeping on the covers, his clothes still on. But there was Scott, lying on the fold-out bed. Awake. Looking at me.

How freaky is that?

It's weird seeing some cunt looking at you when you've just opened your eyes in the morning, it freaks you out. My hand went to my hair, then my eyebrows, cos I thought maybe the cunt had shaved my hair off when I was sleeping, for a laugh. I thought that maybe their plan was to pretend they were sleeping, then once they heard me look at myself in the mirror in the toilet, they'd all piss themselves laughing.

We used to do that all the time, back when there was a dozen of us. No cunt wanted to go to sleep. I remember seeing this film once, some old film, where these guys had found all this gold, and they were around a campfire at the end of the night, and no cunt wanted to go to sleep in case they woke up and some cunt was off with their gold. Well, we'd be like that, except everybody was scared I was gonnae cut off their hair. One year they all made me promise that I widnae cut anybody's hair off, cos they wurnae weans anymore. That's what they said: 'We're not weans anymore,' the lot of them saying it like they were in a union or something. They said they had to go into work on Monday, serious fucking jobs, like Peter in that accountants. So I promised I widnae do it. Then I'd go ahead and do it anyway. The fucking look on their faces. I'd be in fucking knots. If there's one thing funnier than shaving some cunt's hair off when they're sleeping, it's shaving it off after you looked them right in the eye and promised them you widnae do it.

But my hair felt like it was still there. I turned to look at the big mirror on the wardrobe. All my hair was there. Nothing on my face either, no swastikas or cock drawn on my forehead. Nothing. So I looked at Scott and went: 'What is it?'

And he said: 'Can I have my phone?'

That fucking phone. Another day of that phone. No way I was having that.

See, the reason it was pissing me off so much is that Scott is a laugh. You widnae know that, but he really is. He usually is. He's an even bigger laugh than Peter. The cunt's a fucking riot. He's prone to his wee ups and downs, he's probably got something wrong with him, but so's every cunt. And it makes him more of a laugh, when he's up for it. The cunt's wild. But because of all that shite with his maw, he may as well not have been there. I'd almost have preferred it if he wisnae. I'd love to have woken up with my hair all shaved, all bald at the top like Friar Tuck, with him holding a razor and laughing his head off. Instead, I was stuck with this other Scott, with his face tripping him, going like that: 'Can I have my phone?'

I was about to say to him 'She'll be fine', but then I remembered the missed calls. Plus that text that said he was to phone back. But I said, 'It's cool, you've not had anything.'

And he was like: 'Can I just get my phone? I want to check.'

I just said: 'No, I'll check.'

I had his phone under my mattress, in case the cunt tried to check it during the night. I pulled it out and had a look. The two or three missed calls from the night before had shot up to about ten. I had to pure put on this poker face, like there was nothing going on. There were no more texts, though, and I thought that was good, until I thought that maybe it wisnae. Like, whatever they had to tell him was something you didnae just put in a text, d'you know what I mean? But I just went: 'Nope. Nothing.'

He was like that: 'Well, can I just get my phone anyway? Please? Could you please just give me my phone back? Could you? Please?' He kept saying it in this right repetitive way.

Andy stopped snoring. I didnae want the cunt wakening up and jumping in, backing Scott up. So I tried to nip it in the bud. I went: 'Naw, Scott, listen. You're on holiday, mate. They told you they'd get in touch. They hivnae. Just don't think about it. I'll look after your phone. Chill out, mate. C'mon, I came here for a laugh. Don't worry about your maw, she'll be fine.'

I smiled, cos I was 99 per cent sure she wisnae fine, but the smile did the trick anyway.

He went like that: 'Aye, she'll be fine,' sort of in that trance he was in at the airport.

I thought: 'Aye right.'

I looked at Andy, who was starting to wake up. I went like that to Scott: 'Look at this alky cunt. Here, watch this,' and I got up and poured a big glass of water from the tap. Did you know that if you drink a pint of water the morning after getting steaming on ouzo it gets you steaming again? Well, I went like that: 'Hair of the dog,' and chucked it in Andy's face. I think it got a wee smile from Scott, but it might have been because he was biting his nails. Fuck knows.

We got ready and headed down to the pool.

Things were starting to look up. I'd managed to convince Scott that there was a slim chance that his maw was gonnae be alright, and he was nodding in agreement. Andy joined in as well. Scott wisnae back to his usual chirpy self, but at least he was nodding, that was a start. I was feeling good. I asked them all what they wanted to drink and I headed to the bar. A beer for Scott, and a whisky for Andy. I was gonnae forget about Andy's drink on purpose, just to wind him up, but I thought I'd just get it. That's how good I felt.

And I felt even better when I spotted that lassie.

I spotted her from the bar. She was in the pool, the other pool. It's one big pool, really, but there's an island in the middle with the bar on it, making it look like two pools, and the pools are different. The pool that me, Scott and Andy were sitting at was a normal pool, the kind you do lengths in, but then at the end of that is the bar. If you swim around the bar, there's another pool that's more of an oval shape and it's more of a fun pool, with a couple of chutes, and bubbles coming up from the bottom here and there, and currents that push people about.

I was looking at all that, at all the chutes and bubbles and thinking that we should have sat at that pool instead, and that's where I saw her. She was facing my direction, but she wisnae looking at me, she was looking at her mate right in front of her. She was smiling, but she wisnae saying anything, and neither was her mate. And I thought: 'What's that all about?' They wurnae touching each other up or anything, but they were just smiling at each other without saying anything. I worked out what it was, though. It was cos the lassie had spotted me. It was like I looked at her a split second after she'd seen me first, then she'd said to her mate, 'Don't look now, but there's that guy,' and now they were just looking at each other until one of them thought of something to say.

I was gonnae keep looking at her and wait until she looked at me, but I didnae think that would go down too well, especially if I was wrong. Like, imagine if she hidnae spotted me, and she looks up and I'm staring at her. I remembered how weird it was seeing Scott staring at me when I woke up. Except, with a lassie it would be weirder, cos she's a lassie and I'm a guy.

So I looked back to the barman, and I tried hard as fuck not to look back at her. But I told myself that I'd have a wee swim around her way in a minute, once I dumped the drinks.

But then I heard this: 'Oy, Scottish!'

I'm telling you, man, it sent my heart in a wee flutter. It gave me butterflies, like I was coming up on a pill. I looked around, as if I didnae know where it was coming from, then I looked at her, and I acted all surprised.

She was like that: 'Did you not fancy the karaoke then?'

She was treading water, doing a kind of backstroke thing where you don't go anywhere. She had big tits, floating to the top, but I wanted to see her belly. How mad is that? She had a beautiful face anaw, with bits of hair sticking to it. And her smile. It was a friendly smile. It was like she knew me, like she'd known me for ages. I felt like jumping in and shagging her right there and then. But I had to calm it with thoughts like that. I was wearing shorts. They wurnae Speedos, but they were pretty thin, they were shorts for swimming in. You'd be able to spot a semi from a mile off.

I said: 'Aye, we were looking for it, couldnae find it. Well, Andy was looking for it on Google Maps, he's daft about karaokes. What was it called again?'

Her smile got bigger when I was talking to her, she must have really been into the accent.

She went: 'Typically Tropical. That's the new name, though, it won't be on the map.'

I said: 'Oh, now you tell me,' getting kind of jokey cheeky with her. Then I said, 'What did it used to be called?' – just making small talk.

And she went like that: 'Who gives a shit?' Still smiling.

I burst out laughing and went: 'Aye, right enough.'

I really wanted to be with this lassie. I cannae tell you how much. Her patter was right up my street.

Her mate said she was gonnae go and sunbathe, and left the pair of us to it. The pair of us chatted for a bit, asking wee questions, hitting each other with some more jokey cheeky stuff. She slagged off Glasgow, I slagged off London and England in general, shite like that. She was just how I pictured her when I woke up.

I could feel a phone ringing in my pocket. Vibrating. Either mine or Scott's, I didnae know, so I had a quick look. It was Scott's. I felt like chucking it in the water. I'd have been waking up next to that lassie that very fucking morning if it wisnae for Scott and his maw. I felt like firing it right against the tiles of that bar, the way they fire a bottle of champagne against a ship. Fucking b–*dishhhh*!

I just stared at it until it stopped ringing.

She went like that: 'Right, I better go. Are you coming tonight? Foam party.'

I was like that: 'What? Foam party?' A fucking foam party. Wet T-shirts and all that, know what I mean? And she was inviting me. I was like: 'Oh aye. So where is it, where is Typically Tropical? I couldnae find it on my phone, remember.'

And she went like that: 'I thought you said it was your mate's phone.' She was onto me, with this wee smirk on her.

I was like that, pure flustered: 'No, we all checked our phones, just to see if the cunt had typed it in wrong. Honest.'

I shat it when I said 'cunt'. Lassies can have a thing about that, but she didnae say anything. She didnae even blink. She was right up my street.

She told us where the place was. I was to search for some place called the Red Windmill, and Typically Tropical was opposite it. Then she went 'Byyye', and swam away, giving me a wee wave with her foot. I felt my shorts get a bit tighter, I really had to watch it.

Scott's phone rang again. I thought about it for a second. I was gonnae just swipe it to busy, just sweep it under the carpet, deal with it later. But I thought: 'What if she's alive? How good would it to be able to walk over to Scott and say, "She's all clear, mate. Congratulations. The holiday starts here"?'

So I answered it. If I didnae, it would only be a matter of time before they got in touch with Andy. I don't know why they hidnae already. They probably wanted to tell Scott direct, rather than via an alky.

It was his brother Darren, like that: 'Gonnae put Scott on?'

I was thinking: 'Fuck that.'

I said: 'How, what is it?'

But he was like: 'Just gonnae put him on? It's important. I've been trying to get a hold of him since last night.'

I hit him with this bullshit about how Scott just wanted to switch his head off and all the updates were to go through me. Then I went: 'Is she dead?'

He was like that: 'Fuck's sake, Kenny.'

I was like that: 'She is, in't she?'

And he did this big sigh, then he went 'Aye'.

I said, 'Right, I'll let him know,' and hung up.

I had no fucking intention of telling Scott a thing, but when I looked over to Scott, there he was, looking right at me. The cunt was bolt upright on his lounger, sunglasses off, a hand over his eyes to cover them from the sun, so he could get a good look at my face, to try and read it.

I walked over to him, put down the drinks, and I put my hand on his shoulder. And I just went like that: 'All clear.'

So there we were at the foam party.

It was a big fucking place, a big dancefloor on the ground floor and a balcony upstairs. That makes it sound like a club, but it was more like a big disco, with all these neon lights and cheesy tunes, like something out of the eighties. And I was pure looking about for this lassie, but I couldnae see her. I was dying to see her, to actually meet her up close, to stick my arm around her, to give each other a wee push, all that. The pair of us covered in foam.

Scott was looking forward to meeting her anaw. Meeting her mates. He'd perked right up since I gave him the news, so he had. I'll tell you what he was like. Have you ever held a ball under the water, then let it go? I like doing it when I'm in a pool, with a ball or a float or whatever. I get the ball and put it under my feet in the pool, and try to keep it there. Then I let it go. And it floats to the top, quick as fuck like a torpedo. And it disnae just come to the surface, it shoots out the water and flies into the air, splashing your face with water. That's what Scott was like. High as a fucking kite. Jumping about in the foam and hitting it every-where. Andy had his phone out, taking pictures of Scott going mental, all happy for him. But I was getting worried.

Gina G came on, right? 'Ooh Ahh … Just a Little Bit', that one, and Scott went a bit too over the top for my liking. We used to go to this club called Follies, years ago, and they'd play shite like Gina G and dance versions of the Spice Girls. It was shite, we didnae genuinely like it, we were into techno. But see once you got a drink in you? All that cheesy stuff was some laugh.

Scott was like that: 'Follies, Kenny! Follies!', then he started doing this lip sync thing right in front of every cunt, pretending he was Gina G, cunts pure staring at him. He tried to drag me into it, like I was his backing dancer.

But I just went like that: 'Later, mate, later.' I was up for a laugh and everything, but I wisnae up for that. And I wanted him to stop anaw.

See, I hidnae seen that lassie yet, and I didnae want her turning up with her mates, and there's Scott jumping about like a loony. It's alright when there's a dozen of yous, and only one or two of yous are going mental like that. But he was the only other cunt I was pulling with. It was like he was on a pogo stick. It was getting me worried. It's like when I see a good-looking lassie hanging about with two not so good-looking lassies, it makes me wonder what's up with her. You normally get all these stunners hanging about together, they don't want anybody bringing them down. And it makes me think that maybe she isnae a stunner after all, maybe there's something she's hiding. And I didnae want that lassie thinking that about me. I didnae want her thinking, 'Are these the only cunts that will hang about with this guy? What's up with him? Must be something up with him.' I didnae want her getting the wrong idea.

So I went like that to Scott: 'Later, mate, later.'

And guess what the cunt says? He goes, 'Och, fuck ye, then.' And he does this thing with his hand, like he's shooshing me away, like I was a fly. Like I was a fucking fly.

And Andy, who's blitzed, right? Cunt was a wreck. He does this laugh, a big long one, like a cough. It was like the laugh meant: 'Nice one, Scott. That's my boy.'

What d'you make of they cunts?

The cunts that had ruined about three-quarters of the holiday, and they hit me with 'Fuck ye, then' and a big laugh.

But it's cool, man. He who laughs last laughs loudest. It's cool.

Cos his maw was dead.

His maw was dead, and there he was dancing away, unawares. Celebrating. Happy as fucking Larry, bouncing about on the dancefloor to Gina G, unawares that he's killed his maw.

It felt good.

I looked about, to see who was looking at him, thinking to myself: 'If only they fucking knew. If only they all knew that the silly cunt pogoing about has killed his maw and he disnae even know about it, hahaha.'

Then I saw her. The lassie. She was up at the balcony.

She was pretty far away, but I could tell it was her. Her hair was all wetted back, just like in the pool, cos of the foam, and I could make out her tits. It looked like she was wearing some kind of skin-tight white dress, like it was painted on, but it was because she was wearing this soaking wet white T-shirt and it was all stuck to her skin.

A white T-shirt at a foam party. The balls that takes. She was right up my street.

She looked around for a bit, said something to a lassie behind her, then the two of them walked away from the balcony. So I headed for wherever the stairs were, hoping to fuck she didnae look back over and see me scrambling about to find her.

I found the stairs and went up. When I got there, she was back at the fence at the balcony, looking over. I thought her T-shirt was a normal length thing, from what I could see downstairs, but up there I saw that it was a crop top or whatever you call it. She had on a pair of shorts, these shiny things.

And there was that midriff.

She was looking down and to the left, so I went over and stood beside her to her right, so she couldnae see me right away. I stood practically shoulder to shoulder with her, for a laugh, until she noticed me. She eventually got a fright and turned to see who this cunt was standing next to her. I smiled at her and went 'Awright?' – pure putting on the accent a bit, cos I knew she liked it.

She went like that: 'Oh, you prick!' and punched my arm.

It was fucking sore. I was like that: 'Fucking hell.' But it was good. It chilled me out. I thought: 'Here's a lassie who can dish it out.' It makes you less worried about dishing it back. Not that I'd ever hit a lassie, I don't mean that, fuck's sake. I mean patter. All that jokey cheeky stuff we were coming away with at the pool.

She went like that: 'Oh fuck, sorry, haha, didn't mean to hit you that hard,' then gave my arm a rub. And that kicked it off. The rubbing.

She took a step up to me and we started getting off with each other. It was only for about five seconds, but it was long enough for me to put my hand on that waist. I wanted her to know that I liked it, but I didnae want to make it pure obvious, like it was a pure fetish or anything.

I was like that to her: 'So, what is it you do here anyway? You said you work here.'

She said: 'PR. Fancy way of saying I hand out flyers. But I'm finished for the night.'

I didnae know if she was dropping hints or not, but I was dying to whisk her away and shag fuck out her. I was regretting booking us all into that one room.

I said to her: 'Where are your mates, by the way?'

She was like: 'Why?' raising her eyebrows.

I was like: 'Naw, naw, it's for my mate. My mate Scott.'

She was like: 'Oh yeah, what, you thinking of a four-some or summink?'

I didnae know if she was joking or not, but I thought that this was a lassie who was up for a laugh either way. I went like that: 'Aye, a wee four in the bed. Naw, I just mean that we could all get introduced.'

I looked over the balcony to see if I could spot Scott, to shout him up. I couldnae see him right away, cos I was looking into the dancefloor. Then I saw that he had moved. He was talking to Andy. The pair of them were talking at this bit near the toilets that was less busy, a wee empty bit. Andy was holding his phone up to Scott and pointing at it. They wurnae smiling anymore. Scott was shaking his head.

The lassie went like that: 'What one is he, then? I hope it's not the old guy at the hotel. What's he doing with you anyway?'

I said, 'Naw, it's not the old guy.' Then I pointed to Scott and said, 'It's him.'

Just as I pointed down, Scott looked up. The cunt looked up and saw me pointing. You had to see the look on his face. He wisnae pissed off, the look wisnae anger. He looked confused.

I found out later what had happened. It was to do with the pictures that Andy was taking of Scott dancing to Gina G. Andy sent one to Scott's da, to show him Scott celebrating the good news. Scott's da replied, in the way that you can imagine. Then Andy showed Scott the reply.

I felt a bit bad. The way he was looking at me. Jesus. That look on his face. Whatever he was feeling, I widnae wish it on my worst enemy. But then this blob of foam floated down all slowly and landed on his head. And I burst out laughing.

Scott headed for the door. But you cannae blame me for laughing at that, man.

The lassie asked me what I was laughing at, and why my mate was away in a cream puff.

Now, look. See normally? I'd bullshit a lassie that early on. You get folk that urnae up for a laugh, not right away. They get the wrong idea about you, you've got to wait for ages until they see you're an all-right guy, then you can be yourself. It's not really bullshitting, actually, you're just trying to make a good first impression. You fake it. Everybody fakes it. And if you're up against all these other cunts faking it, the lot of them pretending that they don't think this or that's funny when they actually do, and you just come out and be yourself from day one, well, you're gonnae fucking lose. The bird is gonnae think that if that's you trying to make a good impression on day one, what are you gonnae be like when you're being yourself?

But this lassie, though, I got the impression that I could be myself, just like her. Just like her with her belly. So I told her. I told her the lot. The couch. The phone. That bit of foam. And I laughed again.

I thought she'd laugh, but she just went like that: 'You what?' It wisnae cos she didnae hear me, she heard me all right. Her mate came over while I was telling her and asked her if everything was fine, cos of the look on her face. No, she wisnae impressed at all.

What a fucking let-down.

I was gonnae explain to her that it was just patter, it was just banter, it was just something we do, for a laugh. We wind each other up, we take the piss. That's lads.

But I could tell she didnae get it. Some people just don't get it. She reminded me of my maw. That's what she was like. I remember Andy cut my hair once, for a laugh. I wisnae steaming or anything, I was only six. My maw and da had everybody over for Christmas, friends and family, and all us weans, me, Scott, Peter, and a few more. Andy was steaming and he cut this big slice out my fringe with a pair of scissors. I felt fucking stupid, but everybody started laughing, so I started laughing as well. Until I saw my maw. She wisnae laughing. My da was laughing, but she wisnae, and it just brought me right down. Tons of folk are like that.

Laugh, for fuck's sake. Laugh.

I walked out the pub, that Typically Tropical. I just walked away from her. It's shite and everything, but there you go. I walked out and saw Andy running down to the beach to get Scott. The daft cunt was walking into the sea, but we got him out and headed back to the hotel, then we got the flight back the next day, on the Sunday.

The funeral's on Thursday, Scott's maw's. Everybody's meant to be there, all the lads. I've not seen them for ages. Wait till I tell them about that foam. And Scott walking into the water. And the lift.